I0741502

STEVEN WYBLE

Duplicate Minds

A Science Fiction Thriller

SLAUGHTER COUNTY PRESS

First published by Slaughter County Press 2019

This novel is entirely a work of fiction. The names, characters and incidents portrayed in it are the work of the author's imagination. Any resemblance to actual persons, living or dead, events or localities is entirely coincidental.

First edition

ISBN: 978-1-7338008-0-8

This book was professionally typeset on Reedsy.
Find out more at reedsy.com

Contents

One

Rajeev Sundaram's eyes flickered to life and saw only white.

He blinked, but his eyelids felt odd. Nonexistent. Even so, when he closed them, the blinding whiteness blinked out of existence. He kept them closed—the light was nauseating.

What's the last thing I remember? He racked his brain, but it was no use. His mind was foggy and he couldn't think of any reason he'd be . . . wherever he was.

He opened his eyes again. Still nothing but white. But he realized now that he was lying on his back looking up at a clinical white ceiling, like one would find in a hospital.

Maybe he *was* in a hospital. But he didn't remember getting into an accident or having a heart attack. But then again, he wouldn't remember something like that, would he?

He sat up and scanned the room. What he saw appeared to confirm his suspicions. The room's walls were as blindingly white as its ceiling. In front of him sat a stainless steel sink similar to ones he'd seen in hospital rooms; to its right was a door that presumably led to the rest of the hospital. Against the wall to his right sat a small wooden chair with navy blue padding.

There was one peculiarity: Above the door was a circular green light. As Rajeev gazed at the steady green glow, it suddenly began flashing red. He didn't know what that meant, but in his experience, flashing red lights were rarely good things. A wave of panic washed over him, but he suppressed it. Panicking wouldn't help anything and besides, he didn't know for sure what the red light meant. He wasn't going to wait around to find out, though.

His legs felt odd as he dangled them over the edge of the hospital bed. It was like he didn't quite know how to control them. He wondered if he'd been in a coma and his leg muscles had atrophied.

Before he could stand and put his theory to the test, the door swung open and a short, rotund man walked through the door. He carried himself with authority, but his smooth, light-brown skin betrayed his youth. He wore a long, white lab coat, which made Rajeev think he must be a doctor.

The men stared at each other for a long moment, as if each of them were dumbfounded by the presence of the other. The doctor broke the silence.

"You're awake," he said.

Rajeev tilted his head. "No shit."

The words felt strange coming out of his mouth. In fact, his mouth itself felt strange, like he barely had to move it to form the words he wanted to say. And the sound of the words leaving his lips . . . there was a slight buzz to it, like something out of a nightmare.

"What happened to me?" Rajeev asked, a hint of panic creeping into his voice.

The doctor flashed a reassuring smile. His face was cherubic, devoid of facial hair, and he wore a pair of thick-framed black glasses over his chocolate brown eyes. He reminded Rajeev of his brother, Ajay.

"You're in my laboratory at Next Level Technologies," the man said. He pushed his glasses back up his nose as he spoke.

"This is a laboratory? I thought it was a hospital."

The man—perhaps not a doctor after all—nodded.

"It's a medical facility within the laboratory. Uh, let me ask you . . ." He reached into his coat pocket and pulled out a slim device that looked to Rajeev like an oversized, ultrathin tablet. "What's the last thing you remember?"

"Nothing that explains how I got here. I've been trying to remember ever since I woke up. No luck."

The man made a note on the tablet. "That's not surprising," he said without looking up. "But what about your long-term memory? Do you remember who you are?"

"Of course. I'm Rajeev Sundaram."

"Very good . . . and your family? Are you married? Kids?"

"Yeah, I'm married. Have been for twenty-five years, with two kids, a boy and a girl. Listen, I don't mean to interrupt your evaluation, but can you tell me what's going on? I'm still completely in the dark here."

The man looked up from his tablet, a pitying look in his eyes. "I realize this all must be quite disorienting for you, and I apologize. You were gone for a long time."

So he *had* been in a coma. That explained the weird, dissociative sensations he was experiencing. But that left one very obvious question.

"How long was I out?"

At this, the man hesitated. "A very long time. Let's leave it at that for—"

"How long?" Rajeev interjected, his tone insistent.

Again, the man hesitated. His reluctance to answer the question alone made Rajeev's heart sink.

"Stop stalling and tell me how long I've been under. I have a right to know."

The man sighed and nodded. "I'm sorry. It's just . . . as you can imagine, this is difficult. You were in a coma for fifteen years, Rajeev."

Rajeev froze, paralyzed by what he'd just been told. *Fifteen years?* Impossible. That would make him, what . . . fifty-four years old? That would put Sarah somewhere in her late forties. Dev and Mira would both be well out of high school. He brought his hand to his face, but . . . something was wrong with it.

He held the appendage in front of his eyes and marveled at his . . . was that skin? It was rubbery, stiff. *This doesn't look like my arm,* he thought. *Unless my muscles have atrophied . . . it's so skinny.*

"Mr. Sundaram?"

The man's voice broke Rajeev out of his perplexed reverie. He lowered his arm and scrunched his eyebrows in frustration. "There's no way I've been in a coma for fifteen years," he said.

The man gave a knowing look and nodded his head once. "Look, I know it's difficult. But—"

"What's wrong with my arm?" Rajeev interrupted.

"Ah. Yes, about that—"

"I don't feel like myself. I don't feel . . . normal."

"That's not unusual. If I can just explain—"

"Bring me a mirror."

"Mr. Sundaram, if I may—"

"Bring me a mirror, dammit!"

The man sighed, but his face grew stern. "I will bring you a mirror, but not before I have a chance to explain a few things to you."

Rajeev wasn't eager to wait, but he didn't think he had much of a choice. "I'm beginning to think I wasn't in a coma at all."

"You *were* in a coma," the man said, his patience beginning to fray, if only slightly. "You were in a car accident. A bad

4

one. When they brought you into the hospital, you were barely responsive. The doctors managed to restart your heart, but you were comatose."

"For fifteen years."

The man nodded. "For fifteen years."

"And no one tried to pull the plug after all that time?"

"You didn't have a DNR. Your family didn't know exactly what your wishes were and they held out hope you'd come out of it, or that some new medical technology would bring you back."

Rajeev nodded. "But it must have been expensive to keep me here. My family isn't rich."

The man shrugged. "They found a way. And here you are. Their hope wasn't misplaced."

"And yet they're not here. It looks like they've moved on."

"I wouldn't say that. They visited you almost every day, in the beginning. Naturally, the visits dropped off over the years, but they've never stopped coming. You're not allowed visitors currently, anyway."

"But . . . this isn't a hospital. It's a lab."

The man nodded. "That's correct."

"So if I've been in a coma all this time, why am I in a lab and not a hospital?"

The man frowned and crossed his arms. "I've been working my way up to that. One of the things we do here at Next Level is help people in situations just like yours, Rajeev."

The man's insistence on using Rajeev's first name, as if they were best friends and not total strangers, was beginning to wear on his nerves. There was a slight edge to his voice when he spoke next.

"So in fifteen years time, you've figured out how to cure comas, have you?"

The man's face fell. He grabbed the chair, dragged it in front of Rajeev and sat down.

"Not exactly," he said. "Medical science has made some progress in treating comatose patients. But cases such as yours—persistent vegetative states with no apparent end in sight—require more innovative solutions."

"So how'd you wake me up?"

The man's brow furrowed. "Well, that part may be difficult for you to comprehend, given the state of technology at the time of your accident. Specifically, the state of, ah . . . robotics."

"Robotics?"

"Yes. That's our primary area of study." He sighed deeply. "I'll be frank. Things looked bleak for you, Rajeev. Drastic measures had to be taken, and your family figured it was best to—"

"I'm not sure I like where this is going," Rajeev interrupted. He began reviewing all of the odd sensations he'd had since waking up. The disorientation, the difficulty moving, the unsettling feeling that he was having an almost-out-of-body experience . . . it was all pointing toward a reality he didn't want to accept.

"We've developed a technology that gives patients in dire circumstances a second chance," the man said. His words sounded like a rehearsed sales pitch. "When the mind or body is so damaged that conventional medical treatments aren't enough, we've created a way to provide the patient with a new body . . . and a new mind."

A wave of panic shot through Rajeev's body; his mind raced. "Are you saying what I think you're saying?"

The man nodded gravely. "I think so."

"Then say it," Rajeev spat. "Stop dancing around it and tell me outright what you've done."

"Mr. Sundaram . . . we've duplicated your mind, your

consciousness, and placed it in a state-of-the-art roboticized body."

"You're saying I'm a *robot*."

The man nodded. "Yes," he said. "Well, an android, technically. But you're still *you*. It's just your body that's artificial."

Rajeev's mind reeled—whirred? He stretched his arm out before him and studied it. He saw now that the unnaturally rubbery skin that had looked so alien to him was, in fact, rubber . . . or some material similar to it. Now that he knew what he was looking at, he recognized the crude facsimile of the human body for what it was.

"Bring me that mirror," Rajeev barked. "Now."

The man frowned, but retrieved a hand mirror from a drawer below the sink.

"Here," he said, his hand outstretched. Rajeev snatched the mirror out of his hand, but took a deep breath before holding it up to his face. He was sure he wasn't going to like what he was about to see, but he'd have to face this new reality sometime; might as well be now. He lifted the mirror to his face, and gasped.

The face staring back at him wasn't quite human, but neither was it quite what he thought of as robotic. It wasn't metallic, but rather coated in the same rubbery approximation of skin coating his arms. The shape of his face was far flatter than that of any human, and his "eyes" were made up of two oval photosensors. A slight mound served as a nose, but it was nonfunctional—he realized for the first time that he couldn't smell—and his mouth was little more than a thin horizontal slit cut into his faux-skin.

The face staring back at him, he thought, was the visage of a demon.

"I know this is going to take some getting used to," the man said. "I want to assure you that you *will* acclimate to your new body. Everyone always does, and I don't see why you should be an exception."

"I don't see how anyone could get used to living like a tin can."

"You're still you," the man insisted. "You're still Rajeev Sundaram. You're just in a different vessel."

Rajeev shook his head. "I can't wrap my head around this. I'm not sure I'll ever fully comprehend what's been done to me." He looked down at his hands, turning them back and forth, disturbed by how alien they looked and felt. He sighed, the first sign that he was beginning to resign himself to his fate. "So are you a doctor, or what?"

"No. Not in the sense that you mean, anyway. I have doctorates in both mechanical and software engineering."

"That makes sense, I guess. What's your name, anyway?"

The man didn't answer right away. The authority he'd exuded since entering the room suddenly evaporated. He hung his head sheepishly, then raised his eyes to look directly into Rajeev's. "Don't you recognize me?" he asked softly, like a child addressing his—

Rajeev caught his breath—or at least, that's what it felt like, despite his lack of lungs. As he studied the man's face, he knew the realization was correct, and he couldn't believe he hadn't seen it sooner.

"Dev?"

The man offered an awkward smile. "Hi, dad."

Two

He parks the car, but doesn't go inside right away. He's been driving all day and he knows the second he walks through the front door, he will be bombarded. Which isn't an entirely bad thing, but he needs a few moments to himself.

He pulls his phone off its windshield mount and scrolls through his social media feeds. He watches some funny cat videos until he begins to feel guilty for spending so much time alone in the car while his wife and kids are waiting for him inside. He sighs, shoves the phone in his pocket, and gets out of the car.

He avoids eye contact with neighbors as he makes his way to his house. A trash bag rests on the welcome mat, and he grumbles to himself as he grabs it and walks it back to the trash can before returning.

The instant he walks through the door, he's the star of the house. A chubby nine-year-old boy speeds out of the back bedroom and immediately latches onto his leg. "Dad!"

Rajeev chuckles. "Hello, Dev." He tousles the boy's hair, just as a twelve-year-old girl walks toward him, arms outstretched. He hugs her, marveling at how fast she's growing. "Mira, you need to stop growing so much. I'm going to come home from work next week and find out you're getting married and moving out of the house!"

A woman emerges from the kitchen, her hair blonde and curly, her eyes blue and bright, but tired.

"Give your father a minute to himself, kids," she says gently, but with authority. "He's been working all day and needs a moment to rest."

He takes the brief respite as an opportunity to plop himself onto the couch, but he knows the moment won't last. Sure enough, as soon as he's kicked off his shoes, Dev jumps onto the couch beside him, looking up at his dad as if he's his whole world.

"Guess what we did at school today?" he asks excitedly.

"What?" Rajeev asks, trying to muster enough enthusiasm to match his son's.

"We made a computer program!"

"You did! Wow!" He's hamming it up, but he is genuinely impressed; they never taught anything like that when he was in school.

"Uh-huh," Dev says, nodding his head vigorously. "We made a calculator program. It was really cool! I want to be a computer programmer when I grow up."

"That's a good goal, Dev. Computer programmers can make a lot of money. If you study hard, I'm sure you can make your dream come true."

"Really?"

"Yes. If you study, and learn, and work hard, there's no limit to what you can accomplish."

Rajeev's questions were too numerous to count, but Dev insisted they retire to his office before discussing things further. Rajeev tried to climb down from the bed, but struggled to keep his balance. Dev brought his finger to his ear as if he were activating an invisible earpiece.

"Henry, could you please bring us a walker? Thank you."

"A walker? Dev, your old man isn't *that* old."

Dev chuckled. "Remember, fifteen years have gone by. Which

is actually beside the point; technically, you're not even a day old. You've been *reborn*, dad, and it's only to be expected that you'll need to relearn some basic motor functions—like walking."

The door opened and a young man in a white polo shirt and khaki pants wheeled in a steel-gray walker. Dev took the walker and patted the man on the shoulder.

"Thank you, Henry."

"Anything else I can do for you, Mr. Sundaram?"

"That will be all, Henry."

The man nodded and left, and Dev carried the walker over to his father.

Rajeev reached out his arms and curled his new fingers around either handle. With a firm grip, he pushed down on the walker and stood.

He stumbled at first, but Dev helped steady him. He waited until Rajeev had fully regained his balance, then stepped away.

"There's no rush, dad. Take it slow—one step at a time."

Rajeev knew he couldn't do it any other way, even if he'd wanted to. Slowly, he lifted his left foot. It shook and trembled, and would have looked like the leg of someone with Parkinson's disease if it hadn't looked so downright mechanical, like some kind of industrial machine on the fritz. But the walker kept him upright, and he managed to set his foot back on the ground, a little farther than where it had started.

He repeated the process with his right foot, then again with the left, again and again, until he finally made his way across the room and stood directly in front of the door.

"Terrific, dad," Dev said. "You're doing an amazing job—especially so soon after activation."

Activation. Rajeev felt like he was in a fever dream. He offered his son only a low grunt in response.

He shuffled through the doorway and found himself in a hallway that looked far more industrial than the sterile, white patient room would have suggested. The walls, floor and ceiling were all constructed of the same dull gray concrete, and large metal ductwork hung from the ceiling.

"This really *isn't* a hospital," Rajeev muttered.

"No, it isn't. In fact, much of the work we do is for the Department of Defense."

After an agonizing ten minutes of shuffling down the hallway with the walker, Rajeev and Dev found themselves at an elevator. Dev held the door open as Rajeev hobbled inside.

Once the doors slammed shut, Dev reached past his father and pressed his thumb against a pad adjacent to the floor buttons. A green LED lit up when the scan was validated and he pressed the button marked "65"—the top floor.

Rajeev whistled. "All the way on the top floor? You must be pretty high up . . . literally *and* figuratively."

Dev nodded and flashed an awkward smile. "It's my company."

If Rajeev's eyes had been capable of widening, they would have done so. "This is *your* company?"

He was impressed. The boy he remembered—the boy he'd known what felt like yesterday—had been bright and intelligent, but far from ambitious. That wasn't unexpected; young boys goof off and play around with their friends as young boys are wont to do. But clearly there had been a spark in the boy he hadn't noticed if he had created all *this*.

Before his son could explain further, the elevator doors opened. Dev held the door open again and beckoned his father to exit.

"I'll explain everything, but come on out and have a seat first."

The elevator had opened directly into Dev's office. It was a stark contrast to both the sterility of the patient room and the starkness of the hallways.

It reminded Rajeev of the study of an old academic, but with a modern twist. An antique oak desk stood to the right side. An ornate oriental rug was laid out on the hardwood floor. But the walls were bare, and there were only three of them; the fourth, behind the desk, was made up of a floor-to-ceiling window that offered an expansive view of the Chicago skyline. But it wasn't the skyline Rajeev remembered. It was larger . . . taller, taking up more of the empty sky. And it was newer—the skyline of a young, vibrant innovation hub, not the dilapidated, rundown city he'd known all his life.

"Come, have a seat," Dev said, pulling an office chair in front of his desk. He helped his father to it, and then steadied him as he relinquished his grip on the walker and lowered himself onto the chair. Once his father was seated he walked around to the other side of the desk and sat in his own chair.

"So," he said, tapping his fingers against the desktop, "I imagine you have many questions."

"That's an understatement."

"I'll try to explain as much as I can. If you still have questions afterward, I'll do my best to answer them."

"Fair enough. Let's start with the accident."

Dev nodded. "Very well. You were in a motor vehicle accident. It wasn't your fault. A drunk driver swerved into your lane and pushed you off the road."

"Did I have a—"

"A passenger? Yes. They died, unfortunately. The family sued the ridesharing company and received a significant settlement. You survived the accident, but ended up in a coma."

"That doesn't explain the tin-can body."

"Right. I was just getting to that." He clasped his hands

together as he continued. "As I mentioned earlier, you remained comatose for the past fifteen years. But we all held out hope for you, dad. We sold the house to pay for the life support and all your medical care. It bought us a couple years."

"And then what?"

"Having you gone was a huge distraction at first. My grades slipped. I considered dropping out altogether. But it occurred to me that nobody was doing anything to help you, to bring you back to us, and I realized it was up to me. That maybe *I* could find a way to bring you back. It gave me a renewed focus at school. My grades improved and I got a scholarship that paid all my college tuition. That's where I began tinkering with an idea that I thought could help people like you . . . and people like me, with loved ones who were taken from them far too soon."

Rajeev looked down at his artificial body.

"Putting us in tin cans."

Dev tilted his head. "You know, there isn't actually a single ounce of tin in your new body. In fact, most of the outer material is made of silicone."

"I noticed. But you got the color wrong. I look like a white man. Although 'man' is probably too generous."

Dev chuckled. "It's just a prototype. Hence the somewhat unusual look. But as the technology develops, we'll be able to put you in increasingly realistic bodies."

"So explain to me exactly what this technology is."

"Well, I knew I'd never be able to make any headway in the medical field. My natural talents have always been in engineering. So I wondered how I could bring you out of a coma with an engineering solution rather than a medical one. Your brain wasn't functioning properly and because of that, your body was useless as well. To bring you back, I decided I'd have to create not just a new body, but also a new brain."

"But how is that even possible?"

"It wasn't easy. To start, we mapped your brain activity. Although your brain wasn't properly functioning, it served as both the blueprint and the foundation of the new mind we were to create. But because it wasn't completely functional, we had to fill in the gaps. That's where my team and I had to get creative. We began by collecting all the information on you we could—public records, news reports, your personal journals and other writings. We created a bot to crawl your social media and other online activity. We also interviewed anyone we could find who'd known you, from lifelong friends to passing acquaintances. When we'd collected every available piece of data we could find on Rajeev Sundaram, we fed it to a proprietary, machine-learning algorithm that—I'm sorry, I'm going too fast, aren't I?"

Rajeev wondered how his son could tell he'd lost him. He didn't have nearly the same range of facial expression he used to. Maybe his son had programmed a tell into this rust bucket of a body?

"I was following until you mentioned 'machine learning,'" he said. "What is that?"

Dev nodded. "It was a technology in its infancy at the time of your accident, but great strides have been made in the fifteen years since. Basically, we designed an artificial intelligence, an autonomous computer program, that can process information and learn from it, much like humans."

"So you taught this . . . computer person . . . about me?"

"That's the gist of it, yeah. Our AI took the brainscan and used all the data it had gathered to make educated guesses to fill in all the gaps."

"So you made a copy of my brain and then . . . what? What did you do with it?"

Dev frowned. He looked uncomfortable as he answered. "Well, dad, you . . . you *are* that copy."

Rajeev's blood ran cold. No, his—what? Hydraulic fluid? Regardless, his son's words startled and frightened him.

"What do you mean?"

"Our algorithm took what it learned about your mind from the brainscan, filled in the gaps with all the data we'd collected, and spat out a copy of your mind—your consciousness, your *soul*—as close to the original as possible. And that consciousness is *you*. We placed it in the body you find yourself in now."

Rajeev's mind reeled. *No. This isn't possible.* He had memories. Memories of his wife, son and daughter. Of family dinners and vacations. Moments of laughter, anger, reconciliation. These had been real moments—not crude copies, but real experiences that had been etched into the fabric of his soul.

He remembered even farther back: Leaving Mumbai when he was just three years old. The memories were faint, but he remembered walking the bustling city streets with his parents, the smell of hearty street foods, like Panipuri, Vada Pav and Bhelpuri, wafting into his nostrils and making his mouth water, and taxis and rickshaws bustling down the streets. He remembered saying goodbye to it all, boarding a plane with his mother and father and listlessly trying to entertain himself on the seventeen-hour flight to the United States.

These were not counterfeit memories. They were *his*. He remembered them; he'd *lived* them. His son was mistaken or, worse, lying.

"Dad?" Dev furrowed his brow. Rajeev had been silent for nearly a full minute. "I know this must be rather disconcerting news for you. It raises all kinds of ornery philosophical questions—"

"No." Dev's lips clasped tight at his father's forceful exclamation. There was a ferocity to the word that neither of them had expected. But now that Rajeev had verbalized the turmoil taking place in his mind, he couldn't stop. "I know who I am. I'm not some—some *carbon copy* of myself. I know who I am. You're trying to deceive me and it's reprehensible."

"But dad, that's exactly it! You *are* you, *regardless* of whether or not you're a copy. We've proven that here! What does a person truly consist of but their experiences, their memories, their particular way of thinking and perceiving the world around them? We made a copy of all those things and the result is indistinguishable from the 'original' Rajeev Sundaram. You are more tangibly Rajeev Sundaram than the lifeless, unconscious husk on life support at Northwestern Memorial."

"Wait—what?"

Dev fell silent, realizing he'd gotten ahead of himself and revealed too much, too soon.

"Your old body—it was only a vessel, dad. You are so much more than that. All of us are."

"Can I see it?"

There was a beat. "See what?"

"My body."

Dev hesitated. "I thought you were tracking with me. The whole point is that you've moved on to a new body . . . one that may not seem like all that much right now, but is upgradable. Customizable. Your old body is useless."

"I don't expect to go *in* my old body. But I'd like to say goodbye. For closure. You can't know what it's like to have an out of body experience like the one I've found myself in since I woke up."

There was a long silence between them. Dev dragged out his words, as if he didn't really want to be uttering them.

"Unfortunately, as soon as you awakened here, we notified the hospital and told them to take you off life support. Your body is probably on its way to the morgue right now."

"Dammit. I just wanted—"

"You could still see the body," Dev interjected. "It's a bit unusual, but if it would help you attain closure . . ."

"That would be wonderful. Thank you, Dev."

He nodded. "Very well. I'll arrange for a car. Sit tight. I'll get you a wheelchair—you've done enough physical therapy for one day."

When Dev left, Rajeev found himself alone with his thoughts. He was going to the morgue, to see a body. But he didn't consider it his own. Regardless of what Dev had told him, if Rajeev Sundaram's body was really rotting at the morgue, then the original Rajeev Sundaram was truly dead. He, this shadow of the original, may very well be a near-perfect copy of that mind, with the same memories, thought processes, and emotional makeup. But they were not the same. One was the progenitor, the other the offspring. And although the two of them shared a name and a past, from now on, Rajeev would be forging a future of his own.

He was going to bury his father . . . and then start living a new life.

Three

The coroner was captivated by Rajeev's synthetic body.

"Fascinating," he said as Dev helped his father shuffle into the morgue. "Would you mind if I—if I touched it?"

"Don't you dare touch me," Rajeev snapped.

The coroner, a tall, skeletal man who appeared to be in his fifties, jumped. "I'm sorry," he stammered. "I—I didn't realize you were—"

"I don't care. Keep your hands to yourself."

He nodded, and wordlessly beckoned for them to follow him to the back of the building where the bodies were kept.

"I've prepared the body for you here on the examination table," he said. He gestured to the table in the middle of the room. The table—and the body laying on top of it—were covered by a white sheet. "I'll give the two of you some privacy. Just come on out when you're done."

"Thank you," Dev said with a nod. "We won't be long." The coroner left, leaving Dev and Rajeev alone with the corpse of the man who was, in a sense, a father to them both.

Rajeev stumbled toward the table and reached a hand toward a corner of the sheet. "Well . . . shall we?"

"Allow me, dad." Dev grabbed the sheet and pulled it back.

It was a surreal experience, staring into the face of the body Rajeev considered *his*. But that attachment, he reminded himself, was an illusion, born of the memories that had been artificially injected into his mind. Even so, it was startling to see how much the body had changed over fifteen years. It had aged, of course, as evidenced by the numerous wrinkles snaking their way across the face like a network of tiny rivers. But the inactivity of the coma had also affected Rajeev's appearance. His face looked sallow and sunken, devoid of the color and heft one would expect of a healthy, active body. Death played a part in that as well, of course, but he'd only died a couple hours ago. Still, the expression on his face looked peaceful, and Rajeev took some solace in the fact that he had died without pain, never aware of what his family had gone through as they'd waited fifteen years for a miracle that had never come.

Rajeev turned to his son. "Is this difficult for you, Dev?"

He seemed surprised by the question. "It's a bit unsettling, but I made my peace with the situation a long time ago." His lips grew into a wide smile. "Besides—now I have you." He patted Rajeev's back.

"I'm not him. Whatever spark kept him alive has been snuffed out. I'm nothing more than his shadow."

"Perhaps. Perhaps not. As I said earlier, it's a bit of a thorny philosophical issue." His face lit up as he dove into his argument. "There's a thought experiment: Imagine a teleportation device that copies the configuration of *you* down to the last atom. It scans you in, say, LA, then builds an identical copy in New York."

"But what happens to you in LA?"

"Precisely! The original is destroyed—otherwise you'd have a cloning machine. But what if the machine in LA malfunctioned and failed to destroy the original, even after the duplicate has been configured in New York? What do you have then? Is the copy any less *you* than the original?"

"Yes. Because it's still a copy. The original has its own, distinct consciousness apart from that of its clone."

"But if the two consciousnesses are identical to each other . . . well, nevermind. It's a moot point. The fact is, there is now only one Rajeev Sundaram on this earth and you're him."

"Fair enough." Rajeev placed a hand on his progenitor's shoulder. "Goodbye. I'll . . . I'll try to live the life you would have if you'd had the chance." He nodded to Dev, who replaced the white sheet over the body. Then he helped his father as they both exited the room.

* * *

Rajeev's mind wandered on the drive home. He thought of his family. Despite knowing he was only a copy, he couldn't deny the powerful emotions he felt for his wife and children. He'd been reunited with one of them, but he still longed to see the others.

"What now?" he asked Dev. "Can I go home—see Sarah and Mira?"

"I wouldn't recommend that. Not yet."

"Why not?"

"I'd like to take you back to the lab. We've developed a kind of rehabilitation program for new activations to help them acclimate to their new bodies. You've taken to yours surprisingly quickly, but you'd still benefit from some guidance before you venture out into the real world."

Rajeev hung his head. "You'd think I was a toddler and not a grown man."

Dev smirked. "I know, I know. It may seem a bit infantilizing, but truly, this is the best thing for you, dad. When you *do* venture out on your own, you'll barely notice the difference from your old body."

Rajeev looked down at his silicone-covered torso and flashed his son a skeptical look.

"Like I said—we'll get you put into an upgraded model as soon as possible."

Four

B ack at the laboratory, Dev escorted Rajeev to the dormitory that would serve as his home for the next two weeks.

Rajeev pointed to the twin bed stationed in the corner—the only object in the otherwise bare room. "Is that even necessary?"

"Technically, no," Dev responded. "It's meant more as a comfort. We want to make the transition from man to . . . well, *android* . . . as seamless as possible."

"Do I even need to sleep?"

"Yes, actually. Just like a computer gets slow and choppy if it hasn't been restarted in awhile, you'll find it more difficult to process information—to think, essentially—without proper rest."

"Without sleep."

"More or less. We call it 'sleep mode.' It should happen automatically when it becomes necessary. You can help the process along by acting out the sleep rituals you had in your old body—dimming the lights, laying on the bed, closing your eyes . . . err, photosensors. But you know what I mean."

"Well, sleeping is something I've always been good at it. Shouldn't be too difficult."

Dev laughed. "That's the spirit." He patted Rajeev on the shoulder, then headed for the door. "Get some rest. I'll see you in the morning and we'll get you started on physical therapy."

He turned off the light and opened the door, but paused before walking through it. He turned his head to face Rajeev one last time.

"Goodnight, dad. It's really great having you back."

Your father isn't back, Rajeev thought. *He's dead.*

Aloud, he said, "Thank you, Dev. It's good to be back."

* * *

Falling asleep was as easy as Dev had implied, for the most part. It took a bit more conscious thought than Rajeev was used to, but after a bit of mild effort, he found himself unconscious. When he awoke, it was morning.

At least, he assumed it was morning. There were no windows in the room, so all he had to go on was the sense that he had been sleeping for several hours. He wondered what time it—

"The time is five-thirty a.m."

Rajeev jumped, throwing his robotic arms into the air. A man had suddenly appeared out of nowhere, standing by the door. He was skinny, dressed in straight-legged khaki pants and a bright-green polo shirt. His hair was neatly combed and he wore a pair of fashionable, thick-framed glasses.

"Who the hell are you?"

"I'm Daniel, your virtual assistant," the man said.

"My what? Where did you come from?"

"I'm your virtual assistant," Daniel repeated. "I can assist you with things like checking the time or the weather, searching the web, or playing music. I'm fully integrated with the NLT-X4912—"

"The what?"

24

"The NLT-X4912 is Next Level Technologies' fourth-generation artificial body."

Interesting. So apparently Dev had programmed one of these virtual assistants into Rajeev's body. Rajeev remembered virtual assistants from before his accident, but they'd always been confined to little speaker boxes. They'd never looked like real people.

"So you're not real?"

"I was created by software engineers at Next Level Technologies in Chicago, Illinois," Daniel replied matter-of-factly. "My visual appearance is a composite of the engineers who created me."

"So are you a hologram, then? Or what?"

"I exist in your mental interface. No one can see or hear me but you."

"How can I make you go away?"

Daniel smiled. "Just ask."

"Daniel . . . go away."

"Absolutely. See you later." Daniel popped out of existence. But now that he was gone, Rajeev realized Daniel might be able to tell him what, if anything, he should be doing.

"Wait—Daniel? Come back."

Daniel was back before Rajeev could blink. "What can I do for you?"

"Do you know what I'm supposed to be doing?"

Daniel tilted his head like a confused dog. "I'm not sure what you mean."

"Like . . . do I have a schedule or something?"

"Checking your schedule." His face went blank for a few seconds, then he smiled. "You have a physical therapy session scheduled for seven a.m. with M. Schwartz in Suite 1100 on the eleventh floor."

"And before that?"

"You have nothing else scheduled for today."

"Can you send a message to Dev?"

"Let me check your address book." There was a pause. "Would you like to send a message to Dev Sundaram?"

"Yes."

Daniel nodded. "Go ahead," he said. "What's your message?"

"Dev—it's your dad. I don't know what I'm supposed to do until my physical therapy appointment starts."

"Here's your message," Daniel said. He repeated Rajeev's words back to him. "Ready to send it?"

"Yes."

Daniel and Rajeev stared awkwardly at each other. Rajeev's instinct was to make small talk, but he reminded himself that Daniel wasn't a person. In many ways he was more machine than Rajeev was, his newly-acquired robotic body notwithstanding.

After a moment, Daniel mercifully piped up.

"You have a new message from Dev Sundaram," he said. "Would you like me to read it to you?"

"Please."

"Here's the message: 'Good morning, dad. I see you've met Daniel. I should have mentioned him last night but it slipped my mind. Sorry. You can relax until your appointment. Daniel can take you to our entertainment lounge. I'll be there at seven to accompany you to the appointment and make sure you're taken care of.'"

When he was done, Daniel smiled widely at Rajeev. "Would you like to send a response?"

"No, that's okay. Care to take me to the entertainment lounge?"

"Of course. Follow me."

Rajeev stood and established a firm grip on his walker. He

waited for Daniel to move toward the door, but he didn't budge. Rajeev offered an awkward cough, made all the more awkward on account of his lack of a throat.

"I'll need you to open the door," Daniel finally offered. "Remember, I'm not physically present—I'm just in your head."

"Oh, right." Rajeev stepped toward the door. He expected Daniel to move out of the way, but he didn't. He made to nudge him aside, but his hand passed right through him. It was unsettling—like trying to touch a ghost. He reached his hand through Daniel, grasped the doorknob and turned it. As the door swung open, Daniel finally moved, walking out into the hallway.

Daniel walked casually through the hallway as if he were a worker in the company's IT department and not an apparition that existed only in Rajeev's mind. Yet he matched Rajeev's glacial pace perfectly, stopping to wait for him to catch up without a hint of impatience.

They got into the elevator and made their way to the twelfth floor, which was nice—Rajeev wouldn't have far to travel for his physical therapy appointment. When the elevator doors opened, they found themselves standing across from a room with floor-to-ceiling windows in place of a wall. Inside were several pieces of sparse, modern-looking furniture, including several couches and chairs, and a long coffee table. Several people sat on one of the couches, staring at a big-screen television built into the wall.

"Here we are," Daniel said, stepping out of the elevator and beckoning for Rajeev to follow him. Rajeev shuffled along, grasping his walker to maintain his balance.

As they neared the entertainment lounge, Rajeev, after stealing another glance at the people watching the TV, stopped in his tracks, stunned. The people on the couch were like him. *Androids.*

"I'm not sure I want to go to the lounge anymore," he told

Daniel.

"Very well, if that's your wish. But may I ask why you've changed your mind?"

Rajeev didn't remember virtual assistants being so pushy in his day. He didn't feel like explaining himself, but for some reason, he found himself not wanting to disappoint Daniel, as crazy as that sounded.

"I didn't know other people . . . other people *like me* . . . would be here. I'm not sure I'm ready to interact with those things."

"I understand," Daniel said, nodding. "But might I suggest that it could actually be beneficial for you to interact with people who have undergone the same procedure."

Rajeev sighed. "I'm sure it is," he said. "I just don't want to—"

There was something about the way Daniel was looking at him, innocent and naive, that made him seem like an eager-to-please puppy. Again, for whatever reason, Rajeev found himself wanting to avoid disappointing him.

"I'll go in and talk to them for ten minutes," he said. "But after that I think I'd like to go back to my room and wait for my appointment."

Daniel nodded. "Very well. Let's go." He strolled up to a security panel built into the frame of one of the glass panels. He waved his hand in front of it and a small indicator light flashed green. The panel lifted upward into the ceiling and out of sight.

Rajeev made his way into the lounge and three sets of photosensors turned his way and studied him. He was suddenly overwhelmed by embarrassment over the walker. If he'd had cheeks, they would have been flushed.

One of the androids stood and walked up to Rajeev, holding out his hand.

"Looks like you're a newbie," he said, tilting his head at the walker. "Welcome. I'm Ted Ostrom."

Rajeev held out his hand, steadily so as not to lose his balance, and accepted Ted's greeting. "Hi, Ted. I'm Rajeev."

"Rajeev, eh? Sounds Indian."

"It is. I was born in India, but my family moved to the states when I was a kid." Technically, he thought, he had only been born yesterday, but he suspected Ted didn't care about the distinction.

"I only ask out of curiosity," Ted said. "It doesn't really matter. Whatever we looked like in our old lives, we all look the same now."

"Too much so."

Ted laughed. "That's true, but we've been promised that more customization is coming soon."

"So I've heard."

"Of course, we've been hearing that for awhile. But I'm sure it'll be any day now. Anyway, let me introduce you to these guys." He pointed to the android on the right end of the couch. "This is Andrew Lansing."

Andrew gave a salute. "Hey," he said. "Nice to meet you." Rajeev nodded.

"And this," Ted said, pointing to the android on the other side of the couch, "is Natalie Parsons."

Although she looked identical to Rajeev and the other two robotic bodies in the room, she moved in a distinctively feminine manner. "Charmed," she said, a hint of sarcasm in her voice.

"Likewise," Rajeev said. "Say, do you all sound like you did before? How is that possible?"

"I think they make some kind of voice profile based on recordings of you talking," Ted said. "Like they used to do with voice assistants." Daniel perked up as if someone had just mentioned his name.

"Anyway, we were just sitting down to watch a movie together if you'd like to join us," Ted said. "We're only a couple minutes in—we could start it over for you if you like."

"Thank you for the offer, but I just came by to say hello and check out the rec lounge. I'm still getting the lay of the land. I'm sure we'll see each other around, though."

"I'm sure. See you around, Rajeev."

They nodded at each other as Rajeev walked out of the room.

"So?" Daniel asked as they headed back to the elevator. "What did you think?"

"They seemed nice enough." Which was true. But Rajeev didn't add that he found interacting with other androids terrifying. Most of the time he could convince himself he was still in an actual human body and not a woefully inadequate artifice. But interacting with the other androids merely served to remind him of one thing: He was a freak.

Five

D ev knocked on Rajeev's door a couple minutes prior to his physical therapy appointment.

"How'd you like Daniel?"

Rajeev shrugged. "He was fine. A little odd, but I guess that makes sense, since he's not a real person."

"He can be a little off-putting, but he's one of the most advanced artificial intelligences in existence. We're going to release a public version sometime this year. It's going to be tough to break into the market—there's a ton of competition and most of the existing players are far more established than we are—but Daniel is heads and shoulders above them all. I think when people start to realize that, we'll be successful. Anyway . . . are you getting used to your body?"

"When I pretend I'm not in a robotic body, it's mostly tolerable. But whenever I'm reminded of what it is, I feel like I'm on the verge of having a panic attack."

"That's not unexpected, honestly. It's still early. But in a few weeks, you'll barely be able to tell the difference."

Rajeev was skeptical. Besides, how would Dev know? He'd never had his consciousness transported to an entirely new body. It was a completely disorienting experience—one he suspected a person couldn't fully appreciate unless it had happened to them. But it would be pointless to try to explain all that to his son.

"So what happens after this appointment?" Rajeev asked as they walked to the elevator. "Can I go home and see Sarah?"

Dev looked uncomfortable. "Dad, you *have* considered that mom has aged fifteen years, right?"

He had thought about it, but he'd been trying not to. At the time of his accident, Sarah had been thirty-three years old. Now she would be forty-eight. She'd be a different woman now, in appearance, in demeanor, in life experience. She'd be a stranger to him.

And yet, she was his wife. To him, it seemed like they'd embraced just yesterday. She'd been his world, and she *still* felt like his world. But he knew it would not be a seamless reunion. They would be reuniting not as a young man and a young woman, but as a middle-aged woman and a robot. It was like the plot of some kind of twisted scifi sitcom.

"The thought crossed my mind," Rajeev said.

"I don't think mom has quite accepted the fact that you've come back. It might be best to lay low awhile so it can sink in and I can explain to her exactly what to expect. Androids are not an everyday sight yet, you know. Remember, your body is just a prototype. It's never been seen by the public."

"Okay. Well, maybe I can visit Mira, then."

"Mira . . . is very busy, dad. Look, you'll get to see them both eventually, but I think it would be best if you waited. What you need to focus on now is getting acquainted with your new body so you can live as normal a life as possible."

As Dev finished speaking, they approached the physical therapy office, where Rajeev's physical therapist was already waiting for him just outside the door.

"You must be Rajeev," she said. She was a tall, widely-built woman with bright blond hair tied up in a bun. She wore loose-fitting, light-green scrubs.

"Guilty as charged."

She flashed a fake smile and Rajeev intuited that she didn't have much of a sense of humor. She helped him inside and led him to a pair of parallel bars.

"So how exactly does this work?"

"It's not much different from physical therapy for someone who's been in an accident or is recovering from surgery," she said.

"Well I *was* in an accident."

"Right—but not in your current body. You're in a similar boat, though. You essentially have to relearn to walk. It's not a matter of strengthening the muscles used to walk, however, as you don't *have* any muscles. It's more about forging a neural connection between your mind and your body, since neither one is very familiar with the other yet."

"So in other words, it's just a matter of practice."

She smiled. "Basically. Practice makes perfect, as they say—so let's get started."

* * *

After an hour of physical therapy, Rajeev felt he was in somewhat better control of his body—but he still wasn't ready to give up his walker.

Dev invited him up to his office to chit-chat before he had to head off to a board meeting. Dev wheeled his office chair to the other side of his desk, so he and his father could sit across from each other without anything between them.

"I have a surprise for you dad," Dev said, grinning. He walked back behind his desk, opened the bottom drawer, and pulled out a bottle of Scotch and a whiskey glass.

"I don't know if you've forgotten, Dev, but I can't drink Scotch . . . or anything else, for that matter."

"This isn't for you," he replied as he poured himself two fingers' worth of the amber liquid. "It's for me."

"Then what's my surprise?"

"The technology powering your body is still in development, and as such there are many shortcomings. One of them—one many people, dieters in particular, would find a feature and not a bug, however—is the inability to eat or drink. Over the millennia, humankind has come to savor the taste, texture and aroma of food and drink, given its reliance on both. We don't want to deny our patients such human pleasures. To that end, we've developed a variety of products meant to simulate some of the most popular foods and beverages in the country."

Dev walked up to the wall and began pressing buttons that Rajeev hadn't even seen were there. A wall safe popped open. He plucked a small, spherical object out of it, then closed it again.

"This is a prototype. We've done some testing on it and are confident it's safe; we're just putting the finishing touches on it."

"What is it?"

"Here." Rajeev reached out his hand cautiously, and Dev placed the sphere in his palm. "Hold it up to your mouth."

Rajeev brought the sphere up to the mouthpiece he considered his mouth. As it neared, an odd sensation overtook him, mostly in his mind, but also somehow localized to the mouthpiece. It took him a moment to recognize what it was.

"It's Scotch," he said in amazement. "The taste, the aroma—it's all there. I mean, for the most part. It tastes a little off."

Dev let out a self-satisfied chuckle. "It's actually a program that uses near-field communication technology to interact with your mind. This one is for Scotch, but we could make one for pizza, or one for popcorn that could be enjoyed at the movies. We could make one for cotton candy that could be sold at the fair. The possibilities are endless, and as the android population continues to grow, it'll help them have the same kinds of important social experiences surrounding food that they'd have in an organic body."

Dev retrieved his glass off the desk and sat down across from his father.

"I just wanted to be able to enjoy a nice glass of Scotch with my father, now that we're both men."

"One of us more than the other," Rajeev said, and gave his artificial thigh two knocks with his fist.

"You know what I mean."

Rajeev placed the sphere against the mouthpiece. When he withdrew it, he felt dizzy.

"Can this . . . can this actually make me drunk?"

"In a manner of speaking. It simulates the experience, throwing some wrenches in your thought processes. I mean, who drinks alcohol just for the taste, right?"

"It's remarkable." Rajeev lowered the sphere to his lap, as if it were indeed a glass of fine scotch. "I have to say, Dev, I find it amazing that you were able to build . . . all *this*"—he waved his hands around him—"in just fifteen years."

"It wasn't easy. But I was determined."

"You must have been. There's no way you could have done it if you weren't." He hesitated. "It's great to see you have such an amazing professional life, but what is your personal life like? Are you married? Dating? Is there someone special in your life?"

"I've had to make some . . . sacrifices . . . to get to where I am today," he said.

"I'm sorry to hear that."

"I'm okay with it. And besides, I'm not that old. There's still time." He offered a weak smile. "Hey dad . . . I have a random question to ask you."

"Okay. Let's hear it."

"Did I ever tell you about my first kiss?"

"What?"

"I know it's a weird question. I was just reminiscing with some friends the other day about our first kisses and . . . as crazy as it sounds, I couldn't remember mine."

"Dev . . . you were just ten when I had my accident. I don't know that you'd even had your first kiss."

"No, I know, I know. I just thought I might have mentioned it to you at some point is all."

"I'm sorry I can't be more help."

Dev waved his hand dismissively. "It's no problem. Really. It's just that it's sometimes difficult to remember things from my childhood. I guess after your accident I just got so focused on coming up with a way to save you that everything else kind of faded into the background. I mean, I don't even remember simple things like . . . like my favorite place to go on vacation as a kid."

"Well that one's easy," Rajeev said, laughing. "It's just the happiest place on earth."

"Disneyland?"

"Of course! Surely you remember that much. We went when you were six. Every year after that you asked us to take you back for your birthday."

Dev laughed. "Of course. Who couldn't love Mickey Mouse?"

"Well, you were always more of a Goofy fan."

"He's good, too."

Rajeev thought Dev was acting oddly. For the first time since waking up, he felt a chasm between them—the full weight of the fifteen years that separated them suddenly weighed on him.

"I think I'd like to go back to my room now," he said.

"Of course." Dev took one last swig of his whiskey. "I'll escort you back."

Six

Once Dev left the dormitory, Rajeev summoned Daniel.

"How can I help?"

"Daniel . . . can you give me a summary of what's happened in the past fifteen years? I feel like I have a lot of catching up to do."

"Happy to help," he said. "How much detail are you looking for?"

"You can just give me the broad strokes for now."

"Very well."

Much had changed in the past fifteen years, but much had not. People still relied on the internet for information. But it had migrated much more to virtual reality environments and virtual assistants like Daniel, who were built into augmented-reality glasses and sunglasses.

Autonomous vehicles were just becoming a thing at the time of Rajeev's accident, but now they were far more common than the manual variety . . . and the government was making efforts to persuade the few people who still owned the old-school cars to trade them in for autonomous models, which had reduced the traffic death rate to nearly zero. Rajeev had already gotten a taste of this particular technological advancement firsthand on the drive to the morgue.

But there had been no major geo-political upheavals. Peace

still eluded the Middle East, the United States was still run by a two-party system and nuclear weapons were still a visceral, albeit unmentioned, threat. In many ways, the world still looked much as it had fifteen years ago.

Daniel finished his concise overview of the world's fifteen-year history in a little over two hours. That still left much of the day available and little for Rajeev to do.

"You could always go back to the entertainment lounge," Daniel suggested.

The thought of interacting with more of his kind gave Rajeev pause. "I think I'd rather not."

"It's good for human beings to socialize."

"I'm not exactly a human being."

"You are in mind and spirit, if not in body." Daniel offered a reassuring smile.

"Still, I'd really rather not."

"It's completely your choice. I can only make suggestions based on my understanding of what is in your best interest. But I can't make any decisions for you. It's always your choice."

It might have been Rajeev's choice, but Daniel sure was laying on some pressure. He took a moment to think it over and decided another ten minutes couldn't hurt.

"Fine. I'll go for a couple minutes."

Daniel led the way back to the lounge. As they approached, Rajeev saw two androids sitting in chairs, but there was no way to tell if either of them was one of the ones he'd met yesterday.

"Hello," he said as he walked in.

"Hey there . . . Rajeev, right?" It was Ted's voice.

"Guilty as charged."

"Rajeev, you haven't met Brian yet." He gestured toward the other android, then back to Rajeev.

"Nice to meet you," Rajeev said.

"Same to you. So you're a newbie, eh?"

"Newer than you, that's for sure." Rajeev took a seat on the couch, facing the other two androids. "In fact, I had my first physical therapy session today."

"It'll go by in no time," Brian said. "When I was in my old body, I had knee surgery and had to go to physical therapy for months. But in this newfangled thing, I was done in a week."

"That's great. I'm already starting to get a bit cooped up here. I'd like to go see my wife and daughter soon."

Brian whistled. "Don't hold your breath. Not that you have any."

"What do you mean?"

"Do you really think NLT is going to just let you waltz out of here with a piece of equipment worth tens of millions of dollars?"

"What are you saying?"

"These bodies of ours . . . they don't come cheap. And considering that none of us paid for these machines, NLT considers them company property."

Rajeev shook his head. "No. My son told me that after I completed my physical therapy I could go see—"

"I don't know who your son is, but they're probably feeding him the same crock they're feeding us."

Ted placed a hand on Brian's shoulder, as if restraining him. "All Brian's trying to say is that—"

"My son is the founder of the company."

Ted blinked. "Your son is . . . what?"

"He's the founder of Next Level Technologies. This is his company. And he told me I could leave when I was able to walk on my own."

The admission sucked the air out of the room. Brian was the

first to speak.

"I appreciate that your son knows a hell of a lot more than I do what goes on around here," he said. "But anyone capable of becoming one of the richest men in the world within ten years must be able to tell a mighty fine fib or two. Maybe he'll stay true to his word, pull a few strings and let you visit your family, on account of you being his dad and all. But I'm willing to bet he's not going to let a multimillion dollar prototype off company grounds just so you can hug your wife and daughter. I think it's more likely he's feeding you whatever bullshit you want to hear to keep you nice and compliant."

Rajeev stared Brian straight in the photosensors. "Don't you dare talk about my son like that."

Brian shrugged. "I'm sorry. I just call 'em like I see 'em."

"Then you'd better get your eyes checked," Rajeev said. He wanted nothing more than to storm out of the room, but he was still dependent on his walker. As he shuffled out of the room, he dared not turn around to see if the photosensors of the two androids were burning into his back.

Seven

Rajeev sat on the bed in his dorm, fuming.

"Dev is a good boy," he said to Daniel. "I can't believe they'd make him out to be some kind of greedy corporate fat cat."

"He's not a boy anymore," Daniel pointed out.

Rajeev scowled inwardly at the correction, but Daniel was right: Dev wasn't a boy anymore and men, even good ones, often did bad things in pursuit of the greater good. Rajeev doubted Brian's account of his son was completely accurate, but he wondered if there wasn't at least a kernel of truth to it.

"Daniel . . . can you bring up some newspaper articles about Dev?"

"Absolutely. I've gathered the top ten results. Would you like me to read them aloud, starting with the first?"

"Is there any way I could read them myself?"

"Absolutely." As soon as Daniel uttered the words, a newspaper appeared floating in front of Rajeev's face. He reached out to touch it, and it spun in the air.

"It's an augmented reality representation of a newspaper," Daniel said. "You can interact with it. Try holding it."

He reached out a hand and grasped the left edge of it. As he pulled his arm back to his body, the newspaper came with it.

The first article was a profile about Dev in the *Chicago Tribune*.

For the most part, it wasn't anything Rajeev didn't already know. There was some new information about the history of the company, and some of the investment companies that had provided much of the capital needed to grow it into a billion-dollar company. But the rest of the article was the same story Dev had told him when he'd awakened: How a devastating car accident had put his father in a coma when he was just a boy, motivating him to find a way to bring his father back. The article cautioned that such technology was still a ways off, but that Next Level Technologies had made huge strides in the development of robotics and artificial intelligence technologies in the process.

The next article was trash. It appeared to be from some kind of tabloidy blog site and it was all speculation about Dev's sex life—something Rajeev didn't want to think about *at all*.

He moved on to the next one and unlike the other two, it seemed to contain some useful information.

Next Level Versus Fresh Meat: The Race to Upgrade the Human Body

William Stillwell, The Wall Street Journal

Almost as long as humanity has existed, it has sought to cheat death. Conquistador Juan Ponce de León sought the Fountain of Youth. Cleopatra attempted to stave off the ravages of age by bathing in donkey milk. Humankind will stop at nothing to attain immortality.

Thanks to recent technological advances, achieving immortality seems less the stuff of mythology or science fiction and more like an accomplishment that is achievable in our lifetimes. A handful of new companies are on the forefront of the race to create immortal humans, not by reversing the aging of existing bodies, but rather by supplying new bodies that could, at least in theory, be repaired and upgraded indefinitely, granting their inhabitants a kind of pseudo-immortality.

The two most promising companies are different sides of the same coin. Next Level Technologies, the rising robotics and AI firm founded by fresh-eyed billionaire Dev Sundaram, seeks to copy human consciousnesses and implant them into robotic bodies that can be customized and upgraded according to the occupant's wishes. Fresh Meat, a bioengineering firm headed by irreverent whiz-kid Gregory Maltek, is taking a similar, but decidedly different tact. The company is also working on a way to transfer a human consciousness to a new body. Instead of creating artificial bodies, however, the company aims to create biological ones.

Both approaches come with advantages and disadvantages and it's difficult to say at this early juncture which technology will be more widely adopted. It's possible there's room for both technologies; or, the technology could play out similarly to the VHS and Betamax fight, with one technology gaining mainstream acceptance, condemning the other to obsolescence. Either way, analysts agree on one thing: The victor will control a new industry that measures its profits by the billions.

Rajeev hadn't fully understood the ramifications of his son's invention. He'd assumed the primary purpose of these artificial bodies was medical—to help people who had been paralyzed or maimed lead more normal lives. He had been essentially brain-dead himself, which as far as he was concerned was as good as dead. Yet through the technology Dev had developed at Next Level Technologies, he had been given a second chance. Of course, Rajeev saw himself as more of a copy, rather than a continuation, of the original Rajeev Sundaram. But undoubtedly that's not how the general public would view it, especially with the help of some good marketing. But Rajeev's initial impression appeared to be mistaken. Perhaps there was a medical component to Dev's technology, but it was being sold as a form of immortality. That was a different proposition entirely, and one Rajeev wasn't sure he was comfortable with.

In Rajeev's estimation, copying someone's consciousness and then deleting the original was tantamount to murder. No matter how similar the duplicate mind may be to its original, it still cut off the life of the original. It was one thing to use such a method to provide hope to people with no other options—people with fatal illnesses, say, or paraplegics who wished they were dead anyway. But if this technology was being offered to healthy, able-bodied individuals as some kind of anti-aging gimmick, that was an entirely different matter. Would NLT's customers realize the troubling philosophical implications of what they were doing? Probably not—especially if the company managed to get the PR spin just right.

Then there was this company Fresh Meat—apparently NLT's biggest competitor. Their proposed business model seemed to open a whole other can of worms. The thorniest problem Rajeev saw was the matter of supply—where would Fresh Meat get these flesh-and-blood bodies they intended to sell to people? He imagined they'd be grown in a lab with some kind of novel cloning technology he couldn't begin to understand. It reminded him of a Michael Bay movie he'd seen. But the clones in that movie had been fully-realized human beings whose body parts were harvested when the originals needed them. And that raised an important question: Would Fresh Meat's clones have consciousnesses of their own . . . and would the company overwrite them with the minds of its customers? The *Wall Street Journal* article didn't go into much detail, but Rajeev wanted to learn more.

"Daniel . . . can you do a web search for Fresh Meat and display the results in front of me?"

"Yes . . . just a moment." Almost as soon as he uttered the words, the search results were projected in front of Rajeev's face. He scanned through them, looking for any indication of controversy surrounding the company's methods or even any details on how their technology worked. But he came up empty-handed.

"That's all I need for the night, Daniel. Thank you."

"You're welcome. If you need anything—you know how to reach me." In an instant, he was gone.

Rajeev lay down on the bed and contemplated everything he'd learned in the last half hour. He came away with two main facts. The first was that he was embroiled in a burgeoning industry with troubling moral and ethical issues he wasn't sure he wanted anything to do with.

The second was the disconcerting thought that he might not know his son nearly as well as he'd assumed.

Eight

Rajeev awoke the next morning with the same troubling questions on his mind. As his mind cleared, he summoned Daniel to check his schedule.

"You don't have anything scheduled for today—other than physical therapy, of course."

"Could you send a message to Dev asking if he'd care to join me after my appointment?"

"My pleasure. Here's your message—"

"I'm sure it's fine, thank you. Go ahead and send it."

He nodded. "Very well. I've sent the message."

Dev responded a couple minutes later, saying he'd meet Rajeev at the end of his appointment, then take him up to his office where they could talk.

At physical therapy that day, Rajeev found he was making progress. He could walk for a few minutes without his walker, although the longer he pushed himself past that timeframe, the more he began to falter. Brian was right—he should be completely rehabilitated in a week's time, although Rajeev thought "rehabilitated" was a bit of a misnomer, since this was his first go-around in his current body; if anything he was being "habilitated."

As he was leaving the rehab facility he ran into Dev waiting outside in the hall.

"You didn't have to wait out here," he said. "You could have come in and had a seat while I finished up."

"I didn't want to disrupt your appointment. I take it it went well?"

"It went great. I can walk on my own without the walker now . . . a little bit, at least."

"That's great, dad! Care to demonstrate?"

"Ehh . . . I think I'll stick with the walker for now until I make more progress."

"Probably a wise decision."

Dev led him to his office. This time, he sat down behind his desk and offered Rajeev a seat across from it.

"So. What did you want to talk about, dad?"

"I'm making great progress in physical therapy. Like I said, I should be done in less than a week. So I was wondering what the next steps are as far as leaving. I mean . . . what's life going to look like on the other side? I'm not going to be able to work. I'm not going to be able to live a normal life."

Dev's brow furrowed with concern. "Dad, I don't want you to worry about any of that. I know you'll be done with physical therapy soon, but I think it's best if you just stay here for the foreseeable future—for the very reasons you just stated. It won't be too much longer until we're able to get you a better body that's more recognizably human. Besides, if you wait until our androids officially hit the market, all the publicity will make people more comfortable with the sight of someone such as yourself walking around. In fact, you may even turn into something of a minor celebrity—one of the first people to ever undergo this revolutionary procedure."

"That's all well and good, but I'm not asking to move out for good just yet. Can't I just arrange a trip to see Sarah and Mira?"

"Tell you what. Why don't I get in touch with mom and Mira

EIGHT

and arrange for them to visit you here?"

Rajeev wanted to get out of the lab as soon as possible, but he didn't feel he could get anywhere arguing about it. He was beginning to rethink Brian's claims that NLT wouldn't let such valuable tech leave the premises.

"I guess that would be fine."

"Thanks for being flexible, dad. Anyway, I've got a lot of work to get to today. Can I help you with anything else?"

"That's everything. Thanks again for meeting with me."

"Of course. I take it you don't need any help getting to your room, what with all your recent progress?"

"Uh . . . yeah, that's fine. I'll manage." He wheeled his walker onto the elevator and returned to his dorm.

* * *

"I'm growing concerned, Daniel."

Rajeev was sitting upright on his bed, a hand on his chin as he contemplated everything he'd learned in the past two days. Daniel, standing against the wall boasting his near-perpetual smile, tilted his head. "Why is that, Rajeev?"

"I think my son has been led astray by the lure of money. He touts my accident as the impetus behind the founding of this company—and that may well have been his initial motivation. But it's clear he's accumulated a great deal of wealth and power for all his effort and I fear he's become addicted to both."

"As Lord Acton said, 'Absolute power corrupts absolutely.'"

"My fear exactly. But what can I do about it?"

"Dev is your son. Your loved one. You care for him, which means you care about his well-being. If you think he is going down a dangerous path, is it not your responsibility to do something

49

about it?"

"I don't think it's quite that simple."

"Why not?"

"The path he's headed down isn't as demonstrably bad as if, say, he'd become addicted to drugs. Most people would aspire to the same success he's achieved and the continued success he aims to achieve: To change the world, technologically speaking, and accumulate a vast amount of wealth—enough to buy whatever one's heart desires, and to do whatever one dreams of doing."

"But you believe that ultimately the lifestyle he's prioritizing now is to his detriment."

"I believe so, yes. He seems to be putting family on the back burner. I don't think he talks to Sarah or Mira nearly as often as he implies he does. And he's at the age where he should be starting a family, yet the things I saw in the tabloids yesterday . . . well, I don't particularly trust tabloids, but I do believe they tend to exaggerate stories rather than manufacture them out of whole cloth. He may not be a playboy per se, but it's clear he has no intention of settling down anytime soon."

"And you don't think there's anything you can do to set Dev on a better path?"

Rajeev pondered the question. Perhaps it was old-fashioned of him, but he'd always considered himself a family man—not out of a sense of tradition, but rather out of a steadfast belief that a properly-functioning family unit was one of the greatest forces of good in the world. He hadn't always lived up to that ideal, but he'd always strived to. His familial ties to Dev had been prematurely severed after he'd gone comatose, but perhaps Dev could still be steered down the right path through his relationship with his mother and sister.

"Daniel, are you able to look up Sarah and Mira Sundaram's

phone numbers?"

"One moment." There was a pause. "I have the number for one Sarah Sundaram, but I could find no phone records for Mira Sundaram."

That seemed unusual, but maybe Mira had an unlisted number. He was sure Sarah would be able to give it to him.

"So how would I go about placing a call?"

"Outgoing calls are prohibited."

Rajeev couldn't believe what he'd just heard. "Outgoing calls are prohibited? What do you mean?"

"All outgoing communications use Next Level Technologies' network, but you've been blocked from any external communication. You can only call numbers within Next Level Technologies' own network."

"Just me? Or have other people's communications been blocked as well?"

"I can't say. All I know for sure is that yours have been blocked."

Rajeev could somewhat understand his son's reluctance to let him leave to visit his family. It might be a bit of a shock to them to see him as he currently looked. And the fact was, he *did* represent a huge investment on the part of the company and it made sense that they couldn't let him leave without being accompanied by some kind of security.

But blocking his phone calls and other forms of outgoing communication? Not only was it not right, but it seemed suspicious as hell. It seemed Next Level Technologies had become a prison for Rajeev and that meant one thing.

He had to break out.

Nine

He walks down the empty hallways, shaking with anger. It makes it difficult to pay attention to his whereabouts. When he catches sight of a janitor emptying a trash can, he stops and asks for directions to the principal's office. The janitor, a heavyset, red-headed man with dead eyes, simply points in the opposite direction.

Rajeev offers a half-hearted thanks and trudges off in the direction of the janitor's finger. He finds the office, opens the door and sees Mira sitting in a chair in front of the principal's desk. Her arms are folded across her chest and he can't help thinking she looks like a petulant toddler.

He looks up at the principal, an uptight, middle-aged woman with shoulder-length, platinum blonde hair: Mrs. Patricia Hayes.

Principal Hayes meets his gaze and nods. She gestures toward another chair in front of her desk.

"Thank you for coming, Mr. Sundaram. Please, have a seat."

He sits. He turns to Mira and says through gritted teeth, "What have you done, Mira?"

Hayes holds out a hand to stop him. "Mr. Sundaram, it's not as bad as it looks. Mira isn't in trouble per se. We just have some concerns."

"What concerns?"

She nods her head, working her way up to an explanation. "Mira hasn't been paying attention in history class, according to Mr. Yancey.

He's caught her reading books, passing notes, sleeping. She doesn't turn in homework and she has failed the last three tests in a row. She doesn't seem to have this problem in any of her other classes. So, like I said, we're concerned. If she fails history, she'll have to retake it and pass before she can graduate."

Hearing about his daughter's misbehavior feels like a personal assault. Here he is, out on the road every single day to put food on the table and squirrel away some extra money so his daughter can go to college and make something of herself, and she's jeopardizing it all so she can pass inane notes to her friends and catch up on sleep she doesn't need.

"What do you have to say for yourself?" he asks.

She shrugs. "Nothing."

"What do you mean, 'nothing'? You're going to fail history if you don't shape up. What's going on? Or are you just lazy?"

She shrugs again. "Sure, yeah. I'm just lazy, I guess."

"How dare you—"

"Mr. Sundaram," Hayes interrupts, "there's no reason to get upset. Mira is—"

"No reason to be upset? You said she could fail history and not graduate!"

"Yes, but it's not too late. If Mira buckles down, she could squeak by with a D, maybe a C. Even if she fails, she can take summer classes." She pauses to brush her bangs out of her eyes. "I think what we need to focus on is cultivating an environment where Mira can thrive," she continues. "What kind of study environment does she have at home? I can offer some suggestions that would . . ."

Rajeev tries to follow what Hayes is saying, but he finds himself preoccupied with something she'd said earlier: "She doesn't seem to have this problem in any of her other classes." He asks himself, why not?

He pretends to listen to the rest of what the principal has to say, nodding along somberly as if he is deeply invested in what she's saying, but the entire time he's thinking that he needs to speak with his daughter alone.

Finally, she's done speaking and he stands. "Principal Hayes, thank you so much for bringing this to my attention. Rest assured, Sarah and I are going to have a long, hard discussion with Mira when we get home and there are going to be some changes around our house."

"I'm glad you're taking your daughter's education so seriously, Mr. Sundaram. Thanks again for stopping by. I'm sorry it wasn't under more pleasant circumstances."

He nods and leads Mira out of the office. They walk in silence. When they reach the car, they both climb in, buckle up, and stare ahead, trying to pretend the conversation they were just part of never happened. But Rajeev can't pretend and he finally breaks the silence.

"Why are you only having problems in history?"

She turns to look at him. "What?"

"Principal Hayes said you were only having issues in your history class, not in any of your other classes. Why?"

She shrugs. "I don't know, dad. I guess I—"

"Is he touching you?"

"What? Dad, I—"

"Is he touching you inappropriately? Answer the question, Mira."

She seems stunned by the question and Rajeev observes her body stiffening up. "It's . . . it's not what you think, dad."

"Then what is it?"

She sighs, but as she speaks, he can see her body grow looser; she's been holding this in for awhile and it's bringing her some kind of cathartic release to finally get it out.

"Mr. Yancey has never . . . never molested *me, or anything like that. But . . . he'll put his hand on my shoulder sometimes, say,*

if I give a correct answer in class. It's not a big deal, but it makes me uncomfortable. So I stopped answering questions in class. I stopped participating. I just didn't want to give him any excuses to pay attention to me."

In a way, Rajeev is relieved. His daughter isn't lazy. But his rage does not dissipate; it is merely redirected at the pervert he now recognizes Mr. Yancey as.

"Thank you for telling me about this, Mira. I just wish you'd told me sooner." He's going to pull her out of school. Find a private academy—if they can get a scholarship—or even homeschool her if that's what it takes. He won't let her set foot in the same room as that pervert again—and he won't rest until the bastard is fired.

An awkward silence overtakes the car. Rajeev pulls into the driveway and Mira unbuckles her seatbelt, but he places his hand on her shoulder to stop her; he wants to take advantage of the close proximity before she skulks off to her room.

"Mira, you were not in the wrong here. He was. You never have to put up with someone touching you in any way without your permission. You know that, right?"

She looks up, offers a half-smile and nods.

"I do," she says, her voice soft. "I just wasn't sure you would. But I'm glad you do."

One thing Dev had not lied about was that even in this robotic body, and with this computerized mind, sleep was essential if Rajeev wanted to keep his wits about him. So he slept, hopeful that the next morning, feeling refreshed, he could formulate a plan to escape without detection.

Morning came, and he wasted no time.

"Can you pull up the blueprints for the building?"

Daniel shook his head. "I don't have access to that information."

"You must have safety information though, right? How to evacuate in case of a fire, that sort of thing?"

"Yes. There are twelve autonomous drones assigned to the building, each equipped to carry up to four passengers. In the event of an emergency, such as a building fire, the drones station themselves outside windows to carry occupants to safety."

"Twelve times four . . . that's only forty-eight people. There's a hell of a lot more people in this building than that, aren't there?"

"Correct. The drones will return to the building after dropping off their passengers, continuing the cycle until everyone has evacuated."

There were possibilities there . . . start a building fire, evacuate on one of the drones, then take off while everyone's distracted by the chaos. But he couldn't set the building on fire without risking that someone might get hurt, or even killed. He couldn't have that on his conscience. He needed to think of something else.

"That won't work," he told Daniel. "I'm not good at this kind of scheming."

"I'm afraid I'm not much better. As a virtual assistant, my capacity for imagination is limited. Might I suggest, however, that you consult one of the other androids you encountered in the entertainment lounge? They have human minds that may be better suited to 'scheming,' as you put it."

Rajeev scoffed at the idea. He couldn't trust anyone here. For all he knew, the other androids were plants working for NLT.

Then again, Brian was the first one to sow seeds of distrust against the company in Rajeev's mind. If anyone would be happy to help Rajeev escape, it would probably be him.

"Yeah . . . let's take a walk to the entertainment lounge. I have a feeling I might get some inspiration there."

When he got to the lounge, there was only one android inside, sitting on the couch and reading a book—an actual, hardcover book, which had already been somewhat rare in Rajeev's time, before his crash, but which he imagined was almost unheard of in this modern age of LCD screens, augmented reality and holographic projections. And it was doubly weird to see an android reading one.

"Brian?"

The android looked up from its book and shook its head. "Nope. It's me—Natalie.

Natalie. She was one of the androids Rajeev had met after first visiting the lounge. But he hadn't interacted with her at all. He briefly considered asking her the question he'd intended to ask Brian, but he decided it wasn't worth the risk.

"Do you know where I can find Brian?"

Natalie tilted her head. "I do, but I'm not sure I should tell you."

"Why not?"

"Brian said he got the impression you didn't like him much. You're not planning to beat him up, are you?"

"Not at all. I was just hoping to speak to him."

"That's exactly what I'd expect you to say if you were planning to beat him up."

There was a playfulness to her words, but Rajeev was impatient. His first instinct was to ask if she was going to help him or not, but he stopped himself. It would be counterproductive, and besides, there was no reason for him to be so impatient—he wasn't in a hurry.

He sat down in a chair across from her and crossed his legs. "I'm not that kind of person," he said calmly. "In fact, I wanted to see Brian so I could apologize to him. I reacted badly to what he was saying. I didn't need to be so rude."

"Well if you stick around, Brian should be here in about ten minutes. He and Ted are stopping by to watch another movie."

"Oh. Okay." He'd wait, then. But as soon as he made the decision, an uneasy silence settled over the entertainment lounge and Rajeev felt compelled to break it.

"So . . . how did you end up in, you know . . . one of these?" He pointed a finger at his own synthetic body.

"I don't talk about that."

"Oh, I'm sorry. I didn't mean to—"

She laughed. "I'm kidding. I don't mind talking about it. I'll tell you my story if you tell me yours. Deal?"

He nodded. "Deal."

"It was the stupidest thing. I was seventeen and at a pool party with some friends." Her eyes were incapable of conveying the depth of her guilt, but her tone said it all. "I'd had a couple drinks and I did a head-first dive into the pool. I didn't realize it was into the shallow end." She paused, letting the memory saturate her. "I severed my spinal cord at the fifth cervical vertebrae. I was completely paralyzed. The only things I could move were my eyelids and my mouth."

"I'm sorry," Rajeev whispered. "That sounds really rough."

She let out a self-pitying laugh. "That's putting it mildly. I lived like that for thirteen years. For thirteen years, a professional caretaker fed me, bathed me, clothed me. For thirteen years my own body was a prison."

She paused before continuing as if reliving the memories. "About two years ago, someone from NLT contacted my mom. They'd been made aware of my condition—I'm still not sure how; they must have called the hospital, I guess—and said they were working on an experimental procedure that would allow me to move again."

"Weren't you skeptical?"

"Hell no. By that point, I was desperate enough to eat up whatever snake oil anyone was willing to throw my way. My mom was a bit more cautious, but when she discovered that she didn't need to pay a thing—that NLT would actually *pay us* for taking part in the trial—her reluctance melted away. They took me to the lab, put me under anesthesia. I remember falling asleep and then waking up like this." She gestured toward her silicone-covered face. "I was elated at first. I could move my hands, my fingers, my toes. I could turn my head. But then . . ." She trailed off.

"What?"

"I discovered that all I'd done was trade one prison for another."

"What do you mean?"

"They wouldn't let me leave. I wanted to go home, to be with my mother, but it turns out we hadn't read the paperwork we'd signed closely enough. We thought it was just regular old medical liability disclosures and waivers, but it turns out we had inadvertently signed away my freedom. See, NLT owns this body, not me."

"So what Brian was telling me was true."

She nodded her head.

"I was beginning to come to that conclusion anyway," he said. "In truth, that's why I wanted to talk to Brian."

"You planning a mutiny?"

"No." He hesitated to say more, but after what she'd just told him, he thought he could trust her. "I'm planning to get out."

She sat up, taking a sudden interest in his words. "Planning a jailbreak, are we?" She sounded surprised, intrigued and skeptical all at once.

"That's the plan. I need to see my wife and daughter, but Dev won't let me leave. He's blocking my calls to them. He says he'll arrange for them to visit, but I'm pretty sure that's just lip service."

"How do you intend to do it?"

"I'm still trying to figure out the details, but I was thinking of using a distraction."

"Mmmhmm. You think none of us have ever tried that?"

"Uh, well . . . no, I hadn't. But I take it I'm mistaken? How many of you are there anyway?"

"Of *us*—remember, you're an android, too."

"Point taken. How many?"

"There's twelve of us, including you."

"And one of you tried to escape?"

"When I was first activated, there were five of us—I was the fifth. Two of us, Ted and Christian, who I don't think you've met yet, got it into their head that they could distract the guards that are posted twenty-four seven by the entrance and make a run for it."

"That's more or less what I had in mind, but I'm taking it that plan didn't work out so well?"

"No it did not. Christian distracted the guard by pretending to have some kind of meltdown or something while Ted made a break for it. But as soon as he made it out the door, he just . . . froze. He literally couldn't move. He collapsed onto the ground and once the guard got Christian under control, he just got a hand truck, loaded Ted onto it, and wheeled him back inside."

"So there's some kind of failsafe built into the bodies that physically prevents us from leaving?"

"Exactly. So even if you *were* to make it outside, it wouldn't do any good. You'd seize up just like Ted did."

"So we need a new plan."

She snorted. "Good luck with that." She returned to her book and Rajeev meditated on all the new information Natalie had just given him. Escape wasn't an option, apparently. But maybe there was still some way to reach out to Sarah or Mira.

Just as the thought was burgeoning in his mind, the door opened and two androids walked in.

"And you two are . . . ?" Natalie asked, taking in the two identical figures.

"Ted," said the robot on the right, "and Brian." He pointed to his companion.

"Hello, boys," Natalie said. "I was talking to Rajeev here about escape."

"Escaping from your own son's company?" Brian sounded amused. "What changed, Papa Sundaram?"

"Look, I'm sorry about yesterday," Rajeev said. "Family is everything to me and I wasn't prepared to hear what you were saying."

"But now you are?"

"Dev isn't eager to let me off the premises. I owe you an apology. I love my son, but I fear he cares more about money than he does about his own family."

Natalie stood and walked to Rajeev, placing a hand on his shoulder. "Rajeev was just talking about making a break for it before you two came in."

"We've tried that," Ted said. "It won't work."

"I explained that to him."

"She did," Rajeev said, "and I've been trying to formulate a new plan. Maybe we can't escape, but I think we could find a way to communicate with the outside world."

"Yeah?" Brian asked skeptically.

"Yeah. I realize it's not possible to break out of here . . . but how difficult would it be to smuggle something in?"

Ten

There's a bathroom with a window on the fifth floor." Ted sat on the couch in the entertainment lounge. Natalie sat beside him; Rajeev and Brian sat on chairs facing them. "Is it wide enough?" Rajeev asked.

"Should be."

"If not—break it." Brian scanned the eyes of the others, as if daring one of them to challenge him. "Seriously. What are they gonna do? Lock you up?"

Natalie looked grave. "I'm sure they could think up some pretty horrific punishments if we really got out of line."

"Maybe," Brian said, "but I doubt they'll break out the big guns over some shattered glass."

"Okay. I'll get it out, one way or another," Rajeev said. "Ted, you have everything set up here, right?"

He nodded. "Yep. If you can get the bird in the air, I'll handle everything else."

"Excellent." Rajeev stood, nestling a nondescript black box between his hip and arm. "What are we waiting for? Let's do this."

Rajeev headed for the door, leaving the others behind. He stopped just before exiting and took one last look at his co-conspirators. They nodded encouragingly. Rajeev nodded back, turned around and walked out the door.

With an additional three days of physical therapy under his belt, Rajeev was now able to get around without a walker. He was still a bit shaky, but at least he was able to move about unaided.

"Daniel?" The virtual assistant appeared before him, like some kind of spectral apparition.

"How can I help?"

"Daniel, please lead me to the bathroom on the fifth floor."

"Absolutely. Follow me."

Daniel led him to the elevator. After it let them off, he made his way down the hall, took a right down another hall, and then to a bathroom at the end of it.

"Here you are. If that's all you need, I'll give you some privacy."

"Much appreciated, Daniel. Thanks again." Daniel disappeared and Rajeev walked into the bathroom.

Since awakening from his coma, he hadn't set foot in a bathroom. There hadn't been a need to—he didn't eat or drink, which meant he didn't defecate or urinate. This bathroom seemed sparse and clinical, like the medical patient room he'd first awakened in. He spotted the window in the leftmost upper corner of the room and walked over to it. He set the box on the floor beside the sink and reached for the window.

The clasp to unlock it was just barely out of reach. He didn't have toes to stand on, so he just strained his arms. To his surprise, they stretched out just a bit further, enabling him to unlock the window and push it open.

As soon as he turned around, the door opened and a thin, dark-skinned woman walked in. Her hair was up in a tightly-wrapped bun, and she wore a charcoal-gray pantsuit.

"Uh—excuse me," she said, her voice dripping with indignation. "What are you doing?"

Rajeev froze. What an idiot! He must have walked into the

women's bathroom. He was rusty when it came to checking the gender before entering such sensitive facilities.

"Answer me. What are you doing in here?" She looked him up and down. "You . . . *things* . . . don't need to use bathrooms."

Rajeev already had a story ready to go; something about missing the outside world and trying to get a peek of it through the window. "I—I'm sorry," he said. "I was just—"

"You're a *man*?" she shrieked upon hearing his voice. "Get out! Get out *now!*"

Rajeev held out his hands as if deflecting a physical attack.

"I can explain," he said. "I was just feeling a bit claustrophobic on account of—"

"If you're not going to leave, I'm getting security."

"That's not necessary," he said, but she was already out the door. As soon as she was gone, he crouched in front of the box and lifted its lid.

Inside was a six-rotor drone. It felt surprisingly light in his hands. He switched it on and a tiny green LED lit up. He lifted the small aircraft to the window and waited.

"Come on, Ted," he whispered through gritted teeth.

Nothing happened for several moments and then, suddenly, the rotors whirred to life. He let go, and the drone hovered in place a moment before soaring through the window and out of sight.

Rajeev stuffed the black box into the trash can and hurried out of the bathroom, eager to leave before the uptight woman returned with a member of the company's security team.

* * *

On the way back to the entertainment lounge, Rajeev pondered the encounter with the woman in the bathroom. He tried to give her the benefit of the doubt—he *had* gone into the wrong restroom after all—but he couldn't help seeing echoes of the kind of prejudice he'd experienced growing up.

Her words echoed in his mind: "You *things* don't need to use restrooms." Had she forgotten that the minds powering these alien "things" were in fact human—no different from her or any of the other "normal" people working for NLT? How easily people could dehumanize those who seemed different from them. Rajeev had experienced overt racism only a handful of times in his life, but the incidents had been frightening. One stood out in his mind. It was shortly after the September 11 terrorist attack on the World Trade Center. He had been ten, just a boy, and his father had taken him along to the grocery store. As they were walking through the parking lot, an older white man standing a row over began yelling profanities at them. He'd mistaken them for Muslims of Middle-Eastern descent.

The fact that the man had misidentified their race had lessened the blow a bit. But it had been an unsettling experience nonetheless and Rajeev still remembered that sense of dehumanization. It was as if the man had viewed he and his father less like human beings and more like dangerous weapons. He'd seen the same look in the woman's eyes, heard the same fear in her voice. It made him worry about the future of the new class of people that would be created after NLT's technology went mainstream. Would history repeat itself? Would androids be beaten in the streets? Would men and women with hate in their hearts stomp on the computers that made up these people's minds, extinguishing their lives for a second time? At least there was one silver lining—if their minds were backed up on a hard drive somewhere, they could be resurrected for a third, fourth, fifth time . . . they could go on living forever. Or at least, perfect duplicates of them could.

As he approached the entertainment lounge, he observed through the glass walls that his three co-conspirators were gathered around the flat-screen TV. As he walked into the room, they looked up at him expectantly.

"You did it," Natalie said.

"Yeah, but we might have a problem. Some woman walked into the bathroom and—"

"Wait," Brian said, "what was a woman doing in the men's restroom?"

"Uh, well . . . I accidentally went into the wrong bathroom."

All three of them cracked up. "You walked into the *women's restroom?*"

"Yeah, yeah, yuck it up. But the woman who walked in on me said she was notifying security. It's probably just a matter of time before they start checking up on us one by one. So how are you doing, Ted? We don't have a lot of time."

He walked around to take in the view of the TV. As Ted controlled a joystick, the view on the television tracked the path of the drone as it made its way to its destination.

"It shouldn't take too much longer."

The drone had a range of about five miles, which was just barely enough to make it to Sarah's house by Rajeev's estimation. But he wasn't sure how quickly it could make the trip and time was suddenly of the essence.

"I know that park," Rajeev said, pointing to the screen. "It's less than a quarter-mile from the house."

"Yep," Ted said. "Should be just a couple minutes."

True to his word, after just a few minutes, Sarah's house came into view. It was a modest two-story brick building with a small front yard surrounded by a white picket fence.

Rajeev pointed at the screen. "There it is!"

"Where do you want me to land this thing?" Ted asked. "How are we going to get her attention?"

"Can you make it ring the doorbell?"

"I can try."

He brought the drone down to the front door and bumped it into the doorbell, but it didn't hit quite right. Nothing happened. He tried it again; same result. Finally, on the third try, the doorbell rang out.

They waited with baited breath. Rajeev wondered if Sarah was home. A car was parked in the driveway, but that didn't necessarily mean anything. He'd almost given up hope when the door swung open.

It was Sarah. *His* Sarah. She was older than he remembered, yes. There were hints of gray in her blond hair and wrinkles under her eyes. But it was unmistakably Sarah, the woman he'd loved all his adult life. The mother of his children. The love of his life. Melancholy overwhelmed him as he took in her tired visage. He should have been by her side all these years, helping her raise the kids, her constant companion through good times and bad. Instead, he'd left her alone to raise the kids in solitude.

"What the . . . what the hell is going on?" She stared straight into the drone, a look of utter perplexity blanketing her face.

Ted waved Rajeev to his side. "Get over here." He pressed a button on the side of the joystick and motioned for Rajeev to start talking.

"Uh . . . hello," he said.

Sarah's eyes widened and she jumped back. When she spoke, her voice shook.

"Rajeev?"

"Hi Sarah," he said. "We have to talk."

Eleven

Sarah grabbed the drone out of the air and brought it inside. She set it on the kitchen table for her discussion with Rajeev.

He had a lot of explaining to do. He described waking up in Next Level Technologies' laboratory in a robotic body. Contrary to what Dev had told him, she'd had no idea there'd been any effort to duplicate Rajeev's mind and place it in an artificial body. Rajeev got the sense that she understood the philosophical implications . . . that the Rajeev she had known and loved was dead, even if the Rajeev speaking to her through the drone was an incredible approximation of her one-time love.

The conversation then turned to their son.

"I've only spoken with Dev a handful of times in the past two years," she said. "I haven't seen him in person the entire time."

"Wrapped up in his company?"

"I guess. He always says he's too busy whenever I try to get in touch with him."

Rajeev sighed. "That's exactly what I was afraid of. Dev has forsaken his family in favor of pursuing riches. But I know you can get through to him, Sarah."

"I've tried. I don't know what else to do."

Rajeev shook his head. "Well what about Mira? She was always close with her brother."

"She's tried, too."

Rajeev was growing frustrated. "There has to be a way to get through to him."

"Hey," Brian whispered, nudging Rajeev. "Remember to tell her about our imprisonment."

Rajeev nodded. "Hey, Sarah? There's something else. Dev is keeping us here against our will. The company line is that because these artificial bodies are the property of Next Level Technologies, we're not allowed to leave without permission. And if we try to do it anyway, some kind of built-in failsafe stops us in our tracks the second we step outside the building."

Sarah looked horrified. "I'm sorry, Rajeev. I had no idea any of this was going on."

He nodded. "I know you didn't. But we need your help. I don't know how, but you need to get us out of here."

She shook her head despondently. "I have literally no say in the company. Dev owns it all. I can try to talk to him, and I can ask Mira to as well, but like I said, I don't think he'll listen to us."

"Do what you can," Rajeev said. "Keep the drone. We can use it to communicate periodically. It has solar panels, so if you leave it out in the sun from time to time, it'll stay charged."

"Will do. This is all so odd. I just wish—"

A creaking sound cut her off—a door had opened and a voice called out, "Hi, honey. You'll never believe the day I've—"

"I have to go," Sarah hissed suddenly. "I'll be in touch." Then the feed went dead.

None of the androids said a word. Rajeev felt the eyes of the others on him. He could only imagine what they were thinking. *Poor Rajeev . . .*

Of course, they weren't aware that he had been out of Sarah's life for fifteen years. Knowing that, the fact that she'd taken a new lover didn't seem unreasonable. Still, it had come as a bit of a shock. Sarah had remarried, presumably. Maybe it was less serious than that. But the man who had walked in was clearly more than a roommate—he'd called her "honey."

The realization that Sarah had moved on and found someone new to love stung. In a sense, he felt like he'd been with her just a couple weeks ago. But at the same time, he'd already begun disassociating from the life of what he considered the "original" Rajeev. It had also helped seeing the age Sarah had accumulated over the years. She was not the same woman he'd loved. She was undoubtedly far more mature than he was now; his personal growth had stalled for fifteen years.

Everyone stared at him in silence, but he chose not to address Sarah at all.

"We've made contact with the outside world," he said. "That's something."

Natalie nodded. "A first step, hopefully."

"Hopefully," Rajeev agreed. "For now, I'm going to head back to my room. Someone is probably going to come around to each of us with questions about the incident in the bathroom. I'll cop to it. I'll just say I was trying to get some air via the window. Besides, I have some pull—my son owns the company."

They nodded their agreement and Rajeev walked out without another word.

* * *

Sure enough, a security guard came by about an hour later and Rajeev explained what had happened—how he'd tried to explain to the woman why he was in the bathroom and that she hadn't let him get a word in edgewise. And of course, it was a simple mistake that he'd gone into the women's restroom as opposed to the men's, although technically he no longer had a gender.

The guard, a young man who looked to be in his twenties, had a good laugh, but ultimately went on his way. It appeared things had settled back into normalcy. It took just three more days for Rajeev to finish his physical therapy. By the end of it, he was walking almost as fluidly as he had in his old body.

Each night, Rajeev, Natalie, Ted and Brian gathered in the entertainment lounge and streamed the feed from the drone to the TV to see if Sarah had tried to communicate with them. She hadn't.

Rajeev had only communicated with Dev through a series of short voicemail messages courtesy of Daniel, but it was all surface-level conversation. Dev had indicated that he would come congratulate Rajeev on completion of his physical therapy that evening around six, however. Rajeev decided to stop by the entertainment lounge before meeting with Dev. As he approached, he saw one android inside.

"Hello," Rajeev said as he entered. "And you are . . . ?"

"It's me. Ted." He was cradling the drone's joystick in his arms and preparing to stream it to the TV.

"I'm meeting with Dev in about an hour."

"Yeah?"

"Yeah. I'm going to push him to let me see Sarah and Mira."

"You don't think he's going to let you go, do you?"

"I don't think so, but I need to give him the opportunity to prove me wrong."

Ted nodded. "I respect that."

The television flickered to life; he and Rajeev stared at it. Thus far, when Ted had begun streaming the drone's footage, nothing had happened, but now it appeared to be turned on and transmitting footage from Sarah's living room. But there was no one in sight.

"Hello?" Rajeev asked tentatively.

There was silence and then, in the background: "I think I heard something . . . no, I definitely heard something." Sarah's face came into view. Her hair was down, silky and straight, and it looked like she'd carefully applied makeup to her face, which made sense—she'd been caught off guard by her first encounter with the drone, but now she knew she had an audience and wanted to look her best. She picked up the drone and brought it up to her face so that it took up almost the entire frame.

"Hello?" she asked.

"Uh . . . hello," Rajeev said.

"I was right!" Sarah shouted over her shoulder. "He's back."

She backed away from the camera, maintaining a more normal distance, and took a seat. She stared into the camera quizzically.

"Is that really you, Rajeev?"

He laughed. "More or less."

She smiled, but it soon melted into a concerned frown. "I'm sorry about last time. You just caught me off guard and—"

"You don't have to say anything," Rajeev interrupted. She was apologizing for having moved on, but that was nothing to apologize for. "I understand."

"Still, I—"

"No, really. Don't. We have more important things to discuss."

She nodded. "Of course. Speaking of which . . ." She motioned off-camera and a moment later a woman slid into frame beside her. She was widely built, short, and wore her long black hair in a ponytail draped across her shoulder. She wore a pair of oval glasses over her rich, brown eyes.

Rajeev gulped. He knew the instant he laid eyes on her who she was.

"Mira?"

She offered a half-smile that was equal parts joy and wonder. "Dad? Is that really you?"

"It is. How are you, sweetie?"

"I'm fine, dad. How are *you*?"

"Well, I've been better," he said, although even as he said it, he realized that wasn't true; as the second iteration of Rajeev Sundaram, he had been born into captivity—he had, in fact, never been better *or* worse. But of course, this wasn't the time to delve into the philosophy of human consciousness. "I assume your mother has explained the situation to you?"

"Pretty much—you're trapped in Dev's corporate prison?"

"In a manner of speaking, yes. If we try to leave, there's some kind of mechanism built into our bodies that stops us in our tracks. You know—to prevent loss of company property."

She shook her head. "How far my little brother has fallen."

"Mira has some ideas on how to get you out, Rajeev."

"I have a friend who's getting his master's in mechanical engineering from the University of Chicago. I told him about your situation and he thinks it would be possible to disable the failsafe."

"That's great," Rajeev said, "but unless it's something we can do ourselves, or you can smuggle him in here, I don't see how that does us much good."

Mira smiled. "We've thought of that," she said, "and we think we have a plan."

Twelve

I 'm not sure about this," Ted said. "It seems risky."

"Of course it's risky." Brian sounded energized, almost giddy, over the potential for danger. "So what? It's a risk worth taking if it gets us out of this hellhole."

"I'm not sure why *he* gets to be the one to get out of here," Natalie said, nodding in Rajeev's direction. "He hasn't been here for even a month. Most of us have been here for years."

"I don't like it any better than you," Brian said, "but the fact is, Rajeev is the best chance for *all* of us getting out of here eventually. He's the father of NLT's founder and has more leverage with him than any of us do. If he's able to get the ear of the media, he'll also make for a far more compelling story than any of us would—father versus son? It sounds like something out of a soap opera."

Rajeev sat on the couch, doing his best to ignore his compatriots' chatter and steel himself for what they were about to do. By the end of the day he very well may be dead—for a second time. Or he could end up paralyzed, if Mira's friend wasn't as skilled as he seemed to think he was.

He stood. "Let's stop delaying the inevitable and get this show on the road."

They made their way down the hall, single file. Rajeev was struck by the irony that they were given so much autonomy within these walls, yet the second they tried to set foot outside them, they were literally stopped in their tracks. He supposed be should grateful that they were able to move about freely, but he couldn't help but liken their situation to that of prison inmates able to move about the prison facilities freely until they were confined to their cells for the night.

They filed into the elevator and stood silently, side by side, as it lowered them to the first floor. When the elevator doors opened, they marched out and headed for the building's front entrance. Before coming into view of the guards, they huddled up to go over the plan one more time.

"This is crazy," Ted said, a hint of panic creeping into his voice. "This is absolutely nuts. We've tried this. It didn't work."

"It's too late to back out now," Natalie said. "We're in this."

"No," Rajeev said. "We're not going to do this without everyone on board. Do any of you want to back out? It's not too late if you do. We can walk away right now and work out some other plan."

Everyone's face gravitated to Ted. "Ugh, fine," he said. "Let's do it."

Rajeev nodded. "Okay then. On the count of three."

He began counting and as soon as he hit "three," Ted immediately sprinted for the exit.

"Hey!" a guard yelled as he sped past the security station. "Stop!" When it was clear he wasn't going to obey the command, the guard and his companion dashed around the guard station and followed after him. But Ted had a solid head start and was able to make it out the door before the guards could stop him.

The effects were immediate. As soon as he stepped outside, his body seized up. He tipped to the right, falling over onto his side. The guards each picked a side and dragged Ted's body back into the building.

"What were you thinking?" one of the guards asked. "You know you can't leave without authorization!"

"I was just about to leave for the day," the other guard said. "I'm gonna have to stick around at least another hour now filling out paperwork."

Just as they were dragging Ted's body around to the back of the security station, the other three androids barrelled around the corner and made for the exit. It took a moment for the guards to fathom that yet *more* androids were making a break for it. They turned away from Ted and sprinted toward their new targets.

Natalie and Brian turned around abruptly and rushed the guards as Rajeev continued speeding for the exit. The guards had not anticipated that the androids might rush *toward* them, and as they grappled with their opponents, Rajeev made it out the door. He froze and plummeted to the ground. It was a terrifying sensation, knowing that he should be bracing himself for impact but finding himself incapable of doing so. His face was pointed to the ground and all he could see was the dirty pavement. Each second seemed to crawl by at a glacial pace. *Why aren't they here yet?*

Finally, he felt a pair of hands on either side of his body lifting him into the air, accompanied by hushed commands: "Quick! Load him into the van!" Rajeev watched as the pavement gave way to the lush green grass of the lawn, then back to pavement, and finally to the black, rubberized floor of a messy van.

The door slammed shut, and someone shouted, "Go! Go!" The van shot forward and the occupants rocked backward. When it got up to speed, Rajeev's rescuers turned him around on his back so he was facing up. Two faces peered over him: One belonging to a fair-skinned, black-haired sprite of a woman; the other belonging to a widely-built man with short-cropped blonde hair. He looked like a linebacker straight out of a 1950s-era college football team.

"How are you doing, Mr. Rajeev?" the man asked.

"He can't talk, dumbass." The voice came from the front of the van, out of Rajeev's sight.

"Actually, I can talk," Rajeev said. "And it's 'Mr. Sundaram.' Or just Rajeev."

A smug smile crept over the linebacker's face. "Who's the dumbass now?"

"To answer your question, I'm doing fine, although I've been better," Rajeev said. "Is anyone on our tail?"

The woman looked up, out the van's back window. "So far so good."

"If they haven't caught up to us by now, we should be in the clear," the man said. He turned to the driver. "But don't you dare slow down!"

The woman wiped her bangs away from her eyes. "I'm Rosa," she said, then gestured to her companion. "And this is Samuel."

"Pleased to meet you," Rajeev said. "Thank you for rescuing me."

Samuel smiled. "No sweat. Anything we can do to stick it to the man."

"What do you mean?"

"Next Level Technologies," Rosa said. "When we learned what they were doing to you . . . claiming that your body is 'company property.' It pissed us off. It's disgusting. You're human beings. You never asked to be resurrected and squeezed into a body you didn't own."

"Well I'm glad you see things my way. Are you friends with Mira?"

"I am," Samuel said.

"And I," Rosa said, "am her wife."

Rajeev had no way to express his surprise but the pitch of his voice. "Her wife? Oh . . . oh!"

She shot a smirk at Samuel. "Took him a second, but I think he gets it."

"Sorry, I just wasn't expecting—"

"It's okay. We can save formal introductions for later. For now, just relax. We'll get you back up and running in no time."

"Hopefully."

She nodded and flashed him a comforting smile. "Hopefully."

Thirteen

The van pulled up to a nondescript brownstone in a less-than-decent part of town. Samuel slid the door open, then helped Rosa carry Rajeev into the building. The driver and another passenger Rajeev hadn't seen earlier led the way into the building.

They carried him up three flights, then down the hall to the last apartment on the right. The driver knocked on the door and after a moment it opened to reveal a young man with a Mediterranean complexion and hair rolled into tight dreadlocks.

"Damn," he said. "That was quick. Come in." He stood aside as the group marched into the apartment.

"You can set him down here on the couch," the dreadlocked man said. Rosa and Samuel set him down gently, then stepped away to make room.

"Holy crap," the dreadlocked man said, taking in Rajeev's artificial body. "This is remarkable." He crouched above him and slid a hand down the silicone. "Gah! I wish I could tear this off so I could really see the inner workings of—"

"Please don't."

The man jumped. "Right. Sorry. Easy to forget we're working with an actual person here." He retrieved a chair and placed it beside the couch. "I'm Zane and I'm here to help you. I'm getting my master's in mechanical engineering and I know a thing or two about software engineering as well, so between the two, there's at least a chance I can get you moving again. My understanding is there's some kind of failsafe preventing you from moving as soon as you step foot outside of NLT?"

"Correct. Think you can disable it?"

He brought a hand to his chin. "Possibly. It depends on whether the failsafe is something built into the underlying software allowing your mind to communicate with its body, or if it's mechanical. Either one could be a challenge, but I think we'd have better luck if it's a software issue." He grew serious and placed a hand on Rajeev's shoulder. "I feel it's imperative that you understand the risks before we proceed. We're walking into uncharted territory here. This is state-of-the-art, experimental technology and once I start poking around, I don't know exactly what I'm going to find. It's possible that in trying to fix you, I could break you even worse, or wipe you out altogether. If we proceed, I could kill you, Rajeev. Now that you understand the risks, do you still want to proceed?"

"Absolutely."

Zane smiled. "Okay, then. Let's get started."

* * *

Zane found the port that gave access to the underlying software controlling Rajeev's mind and body. It was at the base of his neck, under a silicone flap that protected it from dust and grime. He plugged one end of a cable into the port and the other into his laptop, and spent the next hour sorting through code that looked to Rajeev and everyone else in the room like gibberish.

"Where's Mira?" Rajeev asked, trying to take his mind off the fact that Zane could accidently erase his entire existence with one stroke of the keyboard.

"We told Mira and Sarah not to come," Rosa said. "They're the first people Dev would suspect of helping you escape. In fact, I think he already has a tail on both of them. It's safer for them to stay home and act like they know nothing about this."

"That makes sense. I—"

"Shh!" Zane was suddenly rigid, typing furiously on his keyboard. "I think I found something! If I'm right, you'll be walking again within ten minutes, Rajeev."

"I hope you're right."

"Everyone shut up for a couple minutes and let me concentrate."

The room fell silent, save for the click-clacking of the keys as Zane typed. After a few minutes, he raised a finger into the air.

"If I'm right, once I hit the enter key, you'll be able to move again, Rajeev. You ready for this?"

"Of course!"

Zane lowered his finger and hit "enter." There was a pause and everyone in the room watched with bated breath. For several moments there was nothing. Then Rajeev's right index finger lifted, almost imperceptibly at first, but soon accompanied by his middle and ring fingers. He lifted his right arm, then the left, and propped himself up on the bed. He stood and stuck out his hand to Zane, who accepted and shook it.

"Thank you so much," Rajeev said. "How did you do it?"

"They didn't put much thought into it, really," Zane said. "The bodies are equipped with GPS hardware that pinpoints your location. They implemented a simple program that runs off the data provided by the GPS. As long as you're within the bounds of the NLT campus, it has no effect. But the instant the GPS detected that you'd left, it severed the connection between your mind and body."

"And you deleted the program?"

"No—I left the program intact. I just spoofed your location. As far as the program can tell, you're safe and sound at Next Level Technologies headquarters."

"That's awesome, but . . . if I'm equipped with GPS, doesn't that mean NLT can track me?"

"They can't anymore, because it'll always say you're on the NLT campus. Up until I made the switch, however they would have been able to track your location—which means we all need to leave."

"But what about your apartment?"

Zane laughed. "It's not my apartment, man—we're just borrowing it."

"You broke in?"

"I still prefer to say 'borrowed.' But seriously, we need to split."

Zane gathered his laptop and cables, and everyone filed out the door to the van.

Fourteen

W e're going to take you to my place," Rosa said. "Someone might come looking for you at Sarah's or Mira's."

"I thought you said you and Mira were married."

"We are . . . very recently. I've still got a couple months left on my lease."

"Makes sense. And then we go to the media, right?"

"We're going to record some interviews with you so if we don't get traction with any major media outlets, we can release them ourselves."

"What if none of it goes anywhere?"

"Then we figure something else out. We keep trying until something sticks. Because it's the twenty-first century and corporations shouldn't be allowed to keep slaves, regardless of whether their bodies are made of flesh and blood, or silicon and silicone."

They pulled into the driveway of a single-story, red-brick house that looked like it was built in the fifties. But it had clearly been well maintained, as evidenced by the flawless lawn. As Rajeev approached, the door swung open and there was Mira, dressed in black slacks and a white blouse, staring into her father's photosensors with a look of fascination and confusion.

"Is that really you, dad?"

He was quiet at first, unable to find the words. Finally, he said simply, "Yes."

She stepped forward, opened her arms and wrapped them around him. He wrapped his arms around her and they embraced for a long moment. If Rajeev had had eyes capable of producing tears, they would have been wet.

"I'm sorry for the way I look. It must be unsettling."

She broke the hug and gave her father a chastising look. "I don't care about your appearance. All I care about is who you are on the inside."

In this moment, seeing and holding his daughter for what felt like the first time in years, all distinctions between the "old" and "new" Rajeev melted away. All that was left was a father and a fully grown woman who would forever be his baby girl.

"I love you, Mira. I'm sorry I was away from you for so long."

"It wasn't your fault, dad. You know that."

"I know. Still, I could have driven more carefully. I could have—"

She placed a hand on each of his shoulders and shook him gently as she spoke. "There's no changing the past. You're here and that's all that matters. There's nothing to forgive."

He nodded meekly and they embraced again, until Samuel spoke.

"I'm sorry to break up the moment, but the two of you should get inside just in case NLT has someone hot on our trail."

"What about you?"

"Don't worry about us. We can take care of ourselves. Good luck, Rajeev."

"Thanks for all your help."

"No problem."

Samuel and the others piled into the van, except for Rosa, who stayed behind. The three of them walked into the house and Rosa led them into the living room.

The interior of the house had clearly been remodeled since it was built. Fresh hardwood floors lay beneath their feet. The walls were fresh, pristine and white. The home had an open concept vibe, with a low counter separating the living room from the kitchen.

Mira directed Rajeev to a plush leather recliner in the corner of the room. "Have a seat, dad." As he settled in, she walked with Rosa to the couch and the two of them sat down. Rosa placed a hand over Mira's.

"How long have you two been together?" Rajeev asked cautiously.

Mira stole a glance at her partner beside her and smiled. "We dated for a solid two years and just tied the knot this fall."

Rajeev had always considered himself fairly progressive when it came to such matters, but now that it was his own daughter, he found it a more difficult prospect. He felt ashamed by his own lack of acceptance, but found it was something he could only suppress, not control. He smiled as he struggled to accept the life his daughter had made for herself.

"How did you two meet?"

Rosa answered this time. "Online," she said, smiling broadly. "We met up for drinks. I wanted to keep things casual, but . . . well, your daughter is quite an amazing woman, Rajeev. I couldn't resist her."

"I don't blame you." He looked away awkwardly. "So what now?"

"What's mine is yours," Rosa said. "Make yourself at home. I, uh . . . I assume you won't need to use the kitchen or bathroom, but we have a spare room you can use if you like. Do you sleep on a bed?"

"It's not strictly necessary, but it's what I'm used to."

"Perfect," Mira interjected. "Let me show you to your room, then."

She led him up a pair of slightly creaky stairs to a room at the end of the upstairs hallway. A twin bed took up half of the small room.

"I know it's not much."

"For my purposes, it's great. Thank you."

"So do you actually sleep?"

"Yes. I'm like a computer, apparently. I need to be refreshed every once in awhile."

"Get some sleep then. We'll record some interviews with you tomorrow. It'll turn out better if you're well rested."

"I will. Goodnight, Mira. I love you."

"I love you too, dad. I'm so happy you're back."

With that, she shut the door behind her. Rajeev fell onto the bed and closed his eyes, allowing himself to fall asleep while also reveling in his newfound freedom.

Fifteen

ajeev awoke the next morning to what sounded like fighting. His first thought was that Mira and Rosa were engaged in some kind of spat, but then he recognized one of the voices as male. He jumped out of bed and opened the door to the room.

"Mira?" Rajeev called downstairs. "What's going on?"

He heard the male voice, not addressing him, but, presumably, Mira. "So he *is* here!" Footsteps echoed up the stairs and a man came into view. He stopped halfway up when he caught sight of Rajeev peering down at him.

"Mr. Sundaram . . . it's a pleasure to meet you."

"And you are?"

Mira ran up behind the man and looked up at her father, her eyes pleading for forgiveness. "I'm sorry, dad. He ran past me and I couldn't stop him."

"It's fine, Mira. But the question still stands: Who are you?"

"I'm Donald Lovitz. I work for Fresh Meat."

"Fresh Meat? That . . . that meat suit company? How did you even know I was here?"

He laughed. "Meat suits . . . that's a colorful way of putting it. We manufacture biological body replacements, yes. As for how we found you, well . . . we have our ways, Mr. Sundaram."

"What do you want?"

"Mr. Sundaram, our CEO would like to arrange a meeting with you."

"Gregory Maltek?"

Donald raised an eyebrow. "You've done your research."

"Why does he want to talk to me?"

"I'm afraid I'm not at liberty to divulge that information. Here's what I can tell you. If you accept, we'll send an armored car to pick you up and take you to the airport."

"The airport?"

"To take you to Fresh Meat headquarters in San Francisco."

"So you want me to fly across the country to meet with the head of your company, but you won't tell me why?"

Donald crossed his arms and looked up at Rajeev with the faintest hint of a smile, as if he knew a juicy secret that Rajeev did not.

"How do you like that new body of yours, Rajeev?"

"I like it well enough."

"I'm sure that's all it is . . . sufficient. But what if instead, you could have a body even better than your old one? One that allows you to partake in the pleasures lost to you in a mechanical body? Strolling through a garden and smelling the sweet scents of the flowers. Sinking a fork into a perfectly-prepared steak and letting the juices flow over your tongue, overwhelming you with flavor. Meeting someone special, someone who drives you wild, and ravishing each other after a bottle or two of wine. None of these things are possible for you, Rajeev. But Gregory Maltek can give you all that and more. And if you're willing to help him, he'll give it to you for free."

Rajeev hesitated. He was just as skeptical of Fresh Meat as he was of Next Level Technologies, but in truth, it wasn't lost on him that living in this body meant he would indeed miss out on all the pleasures Donald had just described. As skeptical as he was, the possibility of getting put back into a flesh-and-blood body was tempting. Besides, all that was being asked of him was to meet with Maltek. He wasn't committing to anything and he could always change his mind.

"Okay," he said. "I'll meet with Maltek."

"Dad!" Mira looked shocked. "What are you doing? We have plans for you. You're just going to walk away from all that?"

Rajeev held out his hands defensively. "I'm not committing to anything. I'm just going to talk to the man."

Donald turned around to face Mira. "Honestly, Ms. Sundaram, we'll take good care of him. I promise. We'll even have him back by dinner." He turned back to Rajeev. "I'll send someone to pick you up in about two hours. Be ready." He turned around, nodding at Mira as he passed by, and walked out the door.

As soon as he was gone, Mira marched up the stairs to confront her father. "What are you thinking, dad? Fresh Meat is just as bad as NLT. All they care about is money."

"I'm not interested in their money. I'm just interested in hearing what Mr. Maltek has to say. That's all. I promise I'm not going to become some corporate goon out to do his bidding. Okay?"

She shook her head. "I still don't like this."

"Look, I'll be back by dinnertime, just like he said, and we can start planning our media strategy as soon as I get back."

"All right. I guess I don't really have a choice."

* * *

Rajeev wanted to put on some clothes so he wouldn't attract stares on the way to the airport. Mira's were too large for him, but Rosa lent him a pair of jeans and a black hoodie that did a decent job of covering up the inhuman aberration that was his body.

A couple hours later, there was a knock on the front door. Rajeev answered it, and was presented with a short, frail-looking man with a pug nose and squinty eyes dressed in a driver's uniform.

"I'm here for Rajeev Sundaram," he said.

Rajeev, unsure whether the driver was aware that he would be driving an android and not a human being, tilted his head downward to obscure his face with the hood. "That's me," he said, stepping outside. He followed the driver to the car, and, after the driver opened the door for him, slid into the back seat.

They arrived at the airport, but not at the terminal. Instead, the driver pulled around back to a private runway.

"A private jet?" Rajeev asked.

"Of course. It's actually more cost-efficient for a big company like ours than taking a commercial flight."

Rajeev walked up the steps and into the jet. It reminded him a bit of Air Force One as he'd seen it portrayed in movies. Donald Lovitz was already on board, sitting on a small couch. When he saw Rajeev, he stood and stretched out his hand.

"Glad to see you made it without any problems, Mr. Sundaram. Please, have a seat."

Rajeev shook his hand and took a seat on the couch beside Donald's spot. Donald sat back down as someone pushed the stairs back into the plane and closed the door.

In moments, they were off, soaring into the sky. Donald helped himself to a bottle of beer on the way; Rajeev got the sense that he would have offered him one if he'd been able to partake, but of course, he didn't have a mouth.

The flight took about four-and-a-half hours and Rajeev was grateful when they landed. He realized Donald's promise to have him home by dinner couldn't possibly be true, as it would obviously take just as long for the return trip. Mira was going to be mad. He tried not to think about it.

Another car was waiting for him when he exited the jet. The drive to Fresh Meat took another twenty minutes. The car pulled up to a shiny skyscraper in the heart of the city. The driver parked, got out and opened the door for Rajeev.

"Mr. Sundaram?" A man was waiting for him outside the door. He was tall, square-jawed and handsome, with an impeccable, business-casual haircut and a mouth full of sparkling white teeth. He was dressed in a pinstriped black business suit and wore a narrow, blue tie.

"Yes. I'm Rajeev Sundaram."

"My name is Roger," the man said. "Follow me. Mr. Maltek is very excited to meet you."

Sixteen

Gregory Maltek's office was on the top floor of the sixty-five-story building. Roger led Rajeev into an executive elevator and accompanied him to the top.

When the doors opened, Roger stepped out and gestured for Rajeev to follow him. They walked down the hall, took a left, and then entered through a set of french doors on their left into a spacious office.

A man sat on an ergonomic balance-ball chair behind a desk, typing on his computer. When Rajeev and Roger walked in, he looked up and smiled broadly, standing and walking out from behind the desk to meet them.

"Rajeev Sundaram!" he said. His voice was deep, rich. He looked to be in his early thirties. He wore a white dress shirt without a tie and with the sleeves rolled up to his elbows. He wore a pair of straight-legged khaki pants and a pair of black loafers. "I apologize for the unorthodox invitation, but you're a difficult man to get in touch with." He nodded to Roger. "Thank you for getting him here, Roger. I'll take it from here." Roger nodded and left.

Gregory led Rajeev to a small leather loveseat in the corner of the room. He took a seat in an armchair facing it.

"Why did you bring me here?" Rajeev asked.

"You get right down to business, don't you?"

Rajeev nodded. He got the impression that Gregory Maltek was highly amused by himself, and it annoyed him. But he'd flown all the way out here and it would be a good idea to at least find out why he'd made the trip.

"I gather you're aware," Gregory began, "that my company and your son's company are competing for the same clientele."

"You aren't competing at all, yet. Neither of you actually has a product on the market."

He nodded. "That's true. Neither of us has a product on the market. But that doesn't mean we aren't already competing. Do you remember the format war between Betamax and VHS?"

Rajeev nodded. "I didn't live through it, but I've heard about it, of course."

"The format wars are a lesson in hubris. Sony thought they'd developed a superior format with higher resolution, superior sound and longer-lasting players. And they weren't wrong. Yet the format failed. Do you know why?"

Rajeev shook his head. "I don't."

"It's because they didn't make it for the people—they made it for themselves. They didn't realize that people didn't give a shit about picture quality. The Betamax players were too expensive. VHS players were cheaper and they allowed for longer recording times. VHS was the tape player of the people, and it won out because it met the needs of the people."

"So how does this relate to Next Level Technologies versus Fresh Meat?"

"It's my belief that only one of our respective technologies will win out. So the question is, will people extend their lives by transferring their consciousness into a robotic body, or an organic one?"

"And you undoubtedly expect they'll choose the latter."

"Why wouldn't they? It's the natural choice. People get old and what do they wish for? To be made into a robot—or to be young again? The technology NLT is developing requires its customers to make a trade-off. There's a pro and a con. They get to extend their lives, perhaps even live forever, but as a result they must give up their flesh-and-blood existence and live as a machine incapable of eating, drinking, screwing, or even taking a good shit. Hardly a life worth living."

"It's certainly been an adjustment, but at the same time, I'm not suicidal."

"I'm not saying you are. I'm just saying, I bet you'd be a hell of a lot happier in one of our products than you are in your son's."

"So you flew me out here just to throw that in my face?"

"Not at all. I flew you out here because I need your help."

"With what?"

Gregory sighed. "Think about it in terms of the format wars. The war wasn't without casualties, and Sony wasn't the only one. Think about all the consumers who purchased Betamax players thinking they'd be able to purchase movies for years to come. Their trust was misplaced and they paid a price. In that instance, it wasn't a huge investment. But as you can imagine, immortality won't come cheap. People will likely have to mortgage their homes to pay for it, at least in the early days. What if they bet on the wrong horse? What if they spend tens or hundreds of thousands of dollars on a technology that will ultimately be obsolete in a few years? Wouldn't it be better if the dominant technology were established before it was even on the market?"

"Maybe. But what about choice? What about the free market?"

"The free market is fine and dandy, but if people are bound to be hurt, why not expedite the process?"

"What if they don't choose your product? What if NLT wins

94

out?"

Gregory smiled. "You know, many people argued that in the format wars, the lesser format won. Like I said, Betamax was the superior format in terms of video quality. But what Betamax's champions forget is that nobody cared about video quality. The general public determines the victor with their money. This will be no different. All I'm proposing is that we help people make the right decision. I'm confident people will choose us."

"I still don't see how I fit into this."

"Well, I'd like to have you as an inside man of sorts. Help me gain access to information that could help me more effectively compete with NLT."

"You want me to spy for you."

Gregory smiled, revealing two rows of perfect, white teeth. "Espionage is an essential part of any war. A necessary evil. Now, I know this may strike you as an abhorrent request, to spy on your own son, but I'd argue just the opposite. If the information you provide helps us stamp out the competition, you'll actually be doing the world a service. You'll be ensuring that little old ladies selling their homes for a second chance at life get a true, fully realized life—not a dreary half-life in some rust bucket that could break down at any moment."

"You're forgetting that I'm no longer on speaking terms with Dev. As I'm sure you know, I escaped from the NLT campus."

"Yes, but if anyone can go back, it's you. You're his father. Sure, he'll be pissed. But he'll forgive you. You're family."

"It's not just that. You underestimate the ability of people to make decisions for themselves. And I'm not sure I believe in either one these products. On one hand, you have robotic bodies that sentence their occupants to indentured servitude on behalf of a corporation. On the other hand, you have cloned bodies—bodies that may very well destroy an existing soul as they're readied for new occupants, although I suppose only God knows that for certain."

"I understand your hesitation, Mr. Sundaram, but if I can explain further—"

"My answer is no," Rajeev said firmly. "I won't help you spy on my son's company."

Gregory's smile faded. With a scowl on his face, he said, "But we didn't even discuss your compensation." Rajeev said nothing. He stared blankly at Gregory's suddenly hostile face. "I'm prepared to pay you a hundred thousand dollars. Further, I'm offering to take you out of that tin can and put you back in an organic body. Imagine it, Rajeev—being able to eat, to drink, to make love again. That alone is surely worth more than any amount of money."

Rajeev tilted his head. "Can you tell me more about how you produce these bodies?"

Gregory shook his head. "Afraid not. That's proprietary."

"Then like I said before, I'm not interested." He stood and walked toward the door. Gregory leapt off his seat and blocked his retreat, bringing his face inches from Rajeev's.

"You may want to think long and hard about rejecting my offer," he said. "I have more tricks up my sleeve than you know. And besides, someone you love may need one of my products very soon . . . like your daughter, Mira. Or perhaps your lovely, one-time wife, Sarah."

Rajeev stood there, stunned. Unless he was mistaken, the man had just threatened his family. And for Rajeev, family was everything.

"You're threatening them?"

Gregory stared Rajeev down with eyes that had grown cold and cruel. "I'm not *threatening* anything."

Rajeev sidestepped Gregory and continued walking to the door. As he was about to exit, Gregory called out to him.

"You have twenty-four hours to think it over, Rajeev. After that, all bets are off."

Seventeen

The flight back to Chicago was a solemn one. Rajeev pondered Gregory's threat. How serious was he? Surely it was an empty threat meant to nudge him toward accepting the offer on the table. But what if the threat was real? Fresh Meat was a large company, with enough resources to get away with all kinds of shady business . . . perhaps even assassination.

The jet landed and a car sat on the tarmac waiting to take him home. He thought twice about using the provided transportation, but the fact was, Gregory Maltek already knew where Mira lived. Maybe Rajeev could get Mira and Sarah to lay low for awhile, to move into a hotel. But what's to say Maltek wouldn't track them to their new location?

When the driver dropped him off outside Mira's house, it was dark. Rajeev trudged up the front steps onto the porch and tried to open the door as slowly as possible. He moved slowly, to reduce any noise that might signal his arrival, but it was for nothing: Mira was sitting in an armchair facing the front door, arms folded like a disappointed mother catching her teenage child breaking curfew.

"Back in time for dinner, huh?"

Rajeev shrugged. "I'm sorry. That's what they told me. I didn't think to question it."

"So what did they say?"

He paused. How much should he tell her? On the one hand, Mira didn't like Dev's company any more than he did. On the other hand, she hated Fresh Meat with equal fervor.

"They wanted to see one of NLT's robotic bodies up close," he said. "They offered to put me in one of their organic bodies and pay me for the robotic one so they could study it."

"You refused?"

"Of course."

Mira let out a long sigh. "All right. Well I'm just glad it's over and that you're done with them."

"Me too."

"We'll have to film the videos tomorrow. I'm going to get some sleep. You should too."

"Okay, sweetie. Goodnight. I love you."

"I love you too, dad."

She left for her room. Rajeev didn't move at first. He was preoccupied by the questions and quandaries swimming through his mind. But after several minutes he didn't have a clear answer to any of them and decided a night's sleep might help him think more clearly.

He plodded up the stairs and made his way to the spare bedroom. He took off the hoodie and jeans, folded them and left them on top of the dresser. He took a seat on the bed, not quite ready to lie down and drift off. Light from a streetlight streamed into the room; although complete darkness wasn't strictly necessary for him to sleep anymore, he still found it distracting. He stood and walked to the window to lower the blinds.

He lowered it halfway, then stopped. His eyes had drifted across the street and settled on a nondescript white van with tinted windows parked across the street. He hadn't noticed the van there before. On its surface, it wasn't *that* unusual. People had vans. They parked them on the street.

But Rajeev couldn't get Gregory Maltek's threats out of his mind. *Someone you love may need one of my products very soon.* Gregory knew Mira was staying here with Rosa. It wasn't outside the realm of possibility that the van across the street contained one of his hired goons, his presence designed to intimidate Rajeev into compliance.

No. He was paranoid. He had no reason to think—

Suddenly, the van's headlights lit up and the engine roared to life. It idled for a minute, then pulled into the street and slowly drove away.

It was beginning to seem less and less like a coincidence. Gregory Maltek's threat was seeming less and less benign. Rajeev had come to a conclusion. He didn't like it, but he didn't think he had a choice if he wanted to keep his family safe.

He was going to give Gregory what he wanted.

Eighteen

Rajeev awoke early the next morning, before Mira or Rosa had awakened. He made sure the door to his room was tightly shut, locked it, and took a seat at the foot of the bed.

"Daniel?"

The virtual assistant appeared before him, dressed in the same green polo and khakis, with his familiar grin plastered on his face.

"Hey, Rajeev," he said cheerily. "Long time, no see."

He bristled at Daniel's chatty tone; it felt like it was coming more from the AI's programmers than from the collection of algorithms and code he actually consisted of. Then again, it *had* been awhile since he'd interacted with Daniel; he'd probably be thinking of him as a person again in no time.

"Hi Daniel. Can you send a message for me, please?"

"Absolutely. Who would you like to message?"

"Gregory Maltek."

Daniel paused. "You must have the recipient's contact information in your address book to send a—"

"Check the address book for Gregory Maltek." Gregory hadn't given Rajeev his contact information, but he had a feeling he had already taken the necessary action to ensure Rajeev could get in touch with him.

"Gregory Maltek," Daniel said. "Phone number: Four-one-five, six-two—"

"That's fine, Daniel. Please, send a message to Mr. Maltek."

"Absolutely. What's your message?"

Rajeev sighed. "'I'll do it. Call off your dogs.'"

"Here is your message: 'I'll do it. Call off your dogs.' Would you like to send it?"

"Yes."

There was a pause; Daniel stared ahead blankly.

"Message sent."

It was done. He'd made his choice. He just hoped he could live with it.

A moment later, Daniel announced that Rajeev had received a new message from Maltek.

"Would you like me to read it to you?"

"Obviously."

"'I knew you'd come around. And don't worry—I'll still give you everything I promised. Once you get me the info I need, we'll arrange a time to transfer you into one of our organics.'"

If Rajeev had had a stomach, there would have been a pit in it. Maltek had promised him one hundred thousand dollars and a body that might be worth millions. All it would cost him was his soul.

No. He didn't want Gregory Maltek's blood money. He'd do his dirty work, but only to protect his family. He wouldn't profit from this devious espionage. Maltek would be the only one doing that.

* * *

Mira and Rosa awoke and found Rajeev sitting alone on the living room couch.

"Good morning," Mira said. "What are you up to? You look

bored."

"Not at all. I was just having Daniel read me the news."

"Daniel?"

"My virtual assistant."

"Oh. He's built right into you, huh?"

"Yeah. I was curious about that, actually. Do you have a virtual assistant?"

"I do."

"How do you interact with it?"

She tapped the arm of her glasses. "Augmented reality glasses and a Bluetooth earpiece."

"Makes sense." He turned to Rosa. "What about you? You don't wear glasses."

"I wear AR contact lenses. I don't even have a prescription. I just wear 'em for the tech."

"So what if someone wanted a virtual assistant but they didn't wear glasses or contacts?"

Rosa shrugged. "People still have phones. It's not quite as personal, but it works."

"Anyway," Mira said, "we were just about to have breakfast. I know you can't eat anything, but would you like to join us?"

He shook his head. "I appreciate it, but you two enjoy yourselves. We're going to be spending enough time together today."

He figured he'd go ahead and record the videos with Mira. Then, after she and Rosa had gone to sleep for the night, he'd sneak out and call a car for hire to take him back to the Next Level Technologies campus, where he'd beg Dev for forgiveness and try to get back into his good graces—all so he could spy on his son and his company.

It all felt so treacherous, but he had to remember that it was to protect his family. Maybe not Dev, who had the resources and the personal security to ward off any threat that may come his way, but certainly for Mira and Sarah.

After Mira and Rosa finished their breakfasts, Mira led Rajeev into the living room and directed him to take a seat. A minute later, Rosa came down the stairs with camera equipment under each of her arms. Before long, the pair had set up a backdrop behind Rajeev, and professional lighting to illuminate him. Mira set up a digital camera on a tripod and pointed it at her father.

"Okay," she said. "We're rolling."

"What do you want me to say?"

"Start by stating your name for the record."

"Rajeev Sundaram."

Mira giggled. "No, dad, you have to add the context. You can't just say your name. You have to say, 'My name is Rajeev Sundaram.'"

"Oh, okay. Well, yeah. My name is Rajeev Sundaram."

"Hello, Rajeev Sundaram. Can you explain your . . . well, your rather unusual appearance?"

He looked down, taking in the sight of his own body. Then he looked back up, into the camera.

"Fifteen years ago, I was in a car accident," he said. "It put me in a coma. When I woke up, I was in this body. As you can probably tell, it is not a normal flesh-and-blood body. It's a robotic body made by Next Level Technologies." The conversation was gaining the rhythm of a true interview, with Mira taking on the tone of a real journalist, and Rajeev treating her as such.

"Tell me more about this body of yours."

"According to the company, it's just a prototype. Future models will be more realistic, supposedly. As it is, I can see, hear, speak, and feel. But I can't smell or taste. I don't breathe. It's odd. I don't always feel like myself."

"Are there others like you?"

Rajeev nodded. "On the NLT campus, there were other androids. I don't know how many there are altogether, but all the ones I saw had bodies more or less identical to mine. We had to identify each other verbally, ask each other who we were talking to, because we couldn't tell each other apart visually."

"And could you all come and go as you pleased?"

Rajeev shook his head. "No. We weren't allowed to leave the campus. If we tried, our bodies would seize up and security guards would retrieve us and bring us back."

"If that's the case, then how is it you're here being interviewed, clearly off the NLT campus?"

"I—" He paused, leaning forward and speaking under his breath. "Am I allowed to talk about . . . ?"

"It's fine," Mira said. "Speak freely. If you say anything compromising, we'll just edit it out."

"Okay." He paused before continuing. "A computer program-mer hacked into the system that allows my mind to communicate with its body and disabled the program that paralyzed me if I set foot off campus."

"And why is it that NLT prevented you from leaving their campus is the first place?"

"Because they consider these bodies company property and don't allow them off their corporate campus."

Mira picked up the camera and turned it around to face her. "That's exactly right," she said. "This company holds human beings prisoner—*actual* human beings—inside artificial bodies, hiding behind a shield of intellectual property. NLT thinks we're too stupid and too weak to do anything about it. But they're wrong! Together, we can boycott NLT and force the company to take responsibility for its actions. The only way we're going to enact change is by hitting them where it hurts: their bank account."

Mira turned the camera back to her father. "Rajeev, do you have any kind of special relationship with NLT or any of the company's high-level executives?"

Rajeev hesitated a moment, but then nodded. After all, he'd agreed to this. "Yes," he said. "Dev Sundaram. The CEO. He's my son."

She turned the camera back to herself. "You heard that right. This brave man is the son of none other than Dev Sundaram, the founder and CEO of Next Level Technologies. Dev Sundaram enslaved his own father. What will he do with *your* father, or *your* mother, when he gets his hands on them? Will he promise them immortality, then lock them in a silicon cage?"

She paused. "And guess who I am? I am Mira Sundaram, Dev's sister. Don't get me wrong here. I love my brother. So does my father. We are not against my brother; we are against his actions and the actions of his company. Actions that, if left unchecked, have the potential to allow a corporation to enslave a massive swath of the population. And I'm willing to bet that prospect doesn't sound any more palatable to you than it does to me. And if that's the case, you need to act. Stop purchasing anything with even ancillary ties to NLT—we'll link to a guide in the video description—but also contact your legislators. Tell your senator, your congressperson, your state attorney general, and anyone who will listen that you're concerned about NLT. Tell your lawmakers slavery was abolished more than one-hundred and sixty years ago, and you sure as hell are not going to let it start up again now. Thanks for listening and be sure to like, comment and subscribe and above all else, *share this video!*"

She turned the camera off and set it down, then turned to Rajeev and sighed.

"That's that, I guess."

"It's that good, huh? We got it all in one take?"

"It's good enough. People can smell inauthenticity a mile away nowadays. If we tried to make it flawless, they'd just tune it out."

"So are we going to record more?" Rajeev wasn't sure why he asked it. He knew he wasn't going to be there to record more videos.

"I think this is fine for now. We'll see what kind of response it gets and go from there." She smiled, and Rajeev saw a hint of the young girl he remembered from before his accident. "Thank you for agreeing to do this, dad. It might not make a huge difference, but it will do something. It might just be the straw that breaks the camel's back."

"The camel in this case being your brother."

"Not at all! Just like I said in the video, we're not going after Dev. We're going after his company. It's the company that has corrupted him and not the other way around. I'm just as interested in saving him as I am in saving you and all the other androids NLT has imprisoned."

"I do think he's let greed corrupt him."

She nodded. "He wasn't always like this. He started acting differently one, maybe two years ago. Just out of the blue. One minute he was kind, considerate . . . the next minute he wouldn't return calls from me or mom. Oh, but if he wanted something from us . . . well, then he'd get annoyed if we didn't answer his missed calls quickly enough."

"Sounds like he was overworked."

She nodded. "I'm sure that's part of it. But I think it's more than that. His values became warped. His company became more important than his own family. He goes around giving all these interviews about how he started the company because of how much he loved his family—because he loved *you*, dad—but then, in time, he ends up ignoring the family he still has, like we're nothing."

"I know it's frustrating." He nodded at the camera. "I think all we can do now is tell the truth and hope it does some good."

Nineteen

Mira and Rosa invited Rajeev to join them for lunch, but he pointed out that it would be awkward—he couldn't eat, after all, so he'd just end up watching *them* eat, like some bizarre culinary voyeur—so he politely declined.

He watched as they walked out of the house and into the car. As soon as they'd driven out of sight, he walked upstairs and picked up the clothes he'd left on the dresser. He put them on, walked out of the room and gently closed the door behind him. He ambled down the stairs and went to the front door.

He hesitated, wondering if he should leave Mira a letter explaining where he'd gone, and why. But he decided against it. The less she knew about this debacle, the better. He turned the handle, opened the door and walked out, closing the door behind him.

"Daniel?"

His assistant appeared, standing on the porch in front of him.

"How can I help you today?" he asked cheerily.

"Daniel, call me a car, would you?"

"I'd be happy to, but, uh, you don't have any payment information on file."

"Charge it to Gregory Maltek."

"I'm sorry, I can't—"

"Daniel, send the following message to Gregory Maltek: 'I need money for a car. Please send payment information.'"

"Here's what I have—"

"Go ahead and send it, Daniel."

"Okay. Message sent."

They waited a moment. Rajeev was beginning to get used to these awkward moments with Daniel as he waited for his messages to go through. Finally, the virtual assistant piped up.

"You have a new message from Gregory Maltek. Would you like me to read it?"

"Please."

"'Sure. Payment information is attached for a ten-thousand-dollar line of credit. Consider it an advance.'"

"There you go, Daniel. How about that car?"

* * *

Rajeev had the driver let him off a block away from the entrance to the NLT campus. He didn't want the driver getting entangled in things if there was some kind of confrontation. He thanked the driver and got out.

"Daniel?"

"How can I help?"

"Leave the driver a tip, please."

"Certainly. How much?"

He hesitated, but then remembered the ten thousand dollars in blood money Maltek had made available to him.

"One thousand percent."

"Sir, that's one hundred forty dollars." Rajeev could have sworn he heard a hint of surprise in Daniel's normally flat voice.

"That's fine. Tip the man."

Daniel nodded. "Very well. Tip sent."

As Rajeev approached the double doors that led into the building, a combination of dread and anticipation flowed throughout his body. He wished he could have taken a deep breath, but without a throat or lungs, he just continued on through the doors.

As soon as he entered the building, two guards stationed at the front desk simultaneously did a double take. Then they sprung into action.

Before he could say a word, they were beside him, grabbing either one of his arms and dragging him to their station.

"I—I just wanted to—"

"You're not going to believe this—the missing patient just walked through the front door," one of the guards said into his radio. "Alert Mr. Sundaram."

The other guard stuck a finger in Rajeev's face. "Shut up. Not a peep." Rajeev held up his hands defensively, indicating compliance.

A few moments later, Dev walked down the hall flanked by two additional guards. "Dad?" he asked. "Is that really you?"

Rajeev nodded, and Dev's face grew hard.

"Take him to my office. I'll be there shortly."

The guards affirmed their grips on Rajeev's arms and began dragging him away. Dev stood still, watching Rajeev with eyes that were cold and angry.

* * *

The guards dragged Rajeev into Dev's office and threw him into a chair. Then they waited, arms folded, awaiting their boss.

He arrived a few minutes later, emerging from the elevator with the cold indifference of a movie villain. Rajeev understood how he could be upset with him for escaping, but even so, he couldn't shake the feeling that was not how the Dev he'd known would have reacted. He suddenly felt sad. How would his son have turned out if Rajeev had never gotten into that fateful car accident? What if he'd been there to raise him, to guide him, to teach him what really mattered in life? No, Dev might not have ended up filthy rich like he was now. But in some ways, Rajeev suspected his son would have had a richer life. A fulfilling career with a good work-life balance. A loving wife. Maybe a couple of adoring children. Instead, his son had become a man obsessed with financial success at the exclusion of all else, and he stood before his father now with eyes devoid of love, filled instead with the unmistakable mark of a deep, seething anger over a perceived threat to his growing fortune. Rajeev suddenly lost all confidence that Dev would ever forgive him.

Dev walked directly in front of his father, bending down so they were face to face.

"Welcome back, dad," he said, his eyes narrow, sarcasm dripping off his tongue.

"Glad to be back."

"I'm sure you are." He looked up at the guards and gestured toward the door. "Leave us."

"Hold on, Mr. Sundaram—"

"I said go."

They skulked off to the elevator reluctantly; if they'd had tails, they would have been between their legs. Once they'd entered the elevator and the doors had closed, Dev turned back to his father.

"Where did you go?"

"I went home, Dev. I kept telling you I wanted to see your mother and sister."

"My men went to mother's. She said she hadn't—"

"You didn't really think she'd tell your men the truth, did you?"

"No. But they searched the place and didn't find any trace of you. They searched Mira's place, too, and again: Nothing."

"You can't blame me for going undetected. The fact remains: I left to see my family, which you were denying me the opportunity to do."

"Uh-huh. And how were you able to bypass our failsafe? Did mom help you with that, too?" Rajeev said nothing. Dev took a deep breath and when he spoke again his voice was deep and heavy. "Fresh Meat got to you, didn't they? They want to steal my technology."

The question caught Rajeev off guard and he hesitated for a split second, but then recovered. "Dev, that's . . . that's absurd. All I wanted was to see my family. I asked you repeatedly for a chance to see them and you kept giving me excuses. I decided to take matters into my own hands."

"And decided to figure out how to bypass our failsafe. That's the little detail that condemns you, dad. I know for a fact you don't have the technical prowess to pull something like that off. That means you needed help. The only problem is, you've been in a deep sleep for the past fifteen years. Besides mom and Mira, you don't know anyone—or know how to track down anyone—with the skills to do something like that. But I know Fresh Meat has spies in this company and it wouldn't surprise me at all if they found a way to contact you. I'm sure *they* could pull something like that off."

"I'm sure they could. But in this case, they didn't. And I take umbrage at the assertion that I couldn't have possibly had reason to escape without prodding from a corporation just as corrupt as yours. I wanted to see my family, Dev. Maybe that's difficult for you to understand, the way you've isolated yourself from them, but for some of us, family is still more important than money. And it sure as hell didn't help when I learned that you'd imprisoned not just me, but all these other androids, under the guise of intellectual property rights. We're human beings, Dev, not patents or song lyrics. You've made enemies, not just of competing corporations, but also of good, everyday people who object to your corrupt business practices. It wasn't as difficult for me to find assistance as you might think it was."

"Then why did you come back here?"

"Because you're my son, Dev. I wanted to see Sarah and Mira. And I did. But you're my family, too, and I couldn't just abandon you. I needed to make things right. So . . . here I am."

"We'll see about that. Right now I'm going to need to see exactly how you evaded our failsafe." He walked to a cabinet on the other side of the room, opened it and retrieved a thin tablet computer and a cord. As he walked back to Rajeev, he plugged one end into the tablet and held the other end in his hand.

"May I?"

Rajeev nodded, albeit reluctantly—Dev would undoubtedly reverse the changes Zane had made, which meant he'd be trapped here again, just like all the other androids.

Dev pushed the tip of the cord into the port at the base of Rajeev's neck. He began tapping on the tablet's touch screen, mumbling to himself as he did so.

"Ah," he said suddenly. "I see what they did." He shrugged. "Simple, but effective." He gave the tablet a few more taps, then gave a satisfied sigh. "Well, there we go—back to normal."

Rajeev winced, but then, he'd expected it. He was here to keep his family safe, anyway. He'd be best served to remain focused on that mission.

Dev put away his tablet and when he turned back to his father, his face had softened.

"You always were a stubborn bastard," he said. "You really left just to see mom and Mira?"

He nodded. "Yes."

"I'm still not sure I believe you, but since you're family, I'll give you the benefit of the doubt. But promise me you're not going to pull anything like that again."

"I promise. It was a one-time thing. I'm sorry."

"All right. You can return to your dorm, then."

Rajeev stood and headed for the elevator.

"Oh, and dad?" Rajeev stopped and turned around. "Things have changed around here since your stunt. Don't expect to have the same freedoms you had before."

Rajeev gave a short, curt nod and continued to the elevator.

Twenty

Instead of going straight to his dorm, Rajeev found himself heading to the entertainment lounge instead. Although he'd been gone only a few days, he was surprised to find he missed the motley crew of androids who had helped him escape. He barely knew them, but they'd been bonded by circumstance, each of them imprisoned in corporate-owned artificial bodies that made them look like monsters. They were freaks, and all they had in this corporate wasteland was each other.

At the same time, he was nervous to face them. After all, he'd left as their supposed savior, escaping the confines of this prison to find help for those he'd left behind. The only thing they would find more dispiriting than him never returning was him returning empty-handed, without a single morsel of hope for them. And that's exactly how he was returning now.

As he approached the glass walls, he made out a sole occupant—an android sitting on the couch, legs crossed, engrossed in a worn paperback book.

He opened the door and crept in quietly. The android failed to look up, and Rajeev wondered whether it was because it didn't notice he'd entered, or didn't care.

"Hi," he said. "And you are . . . ?"

The android looked up from the book, but did not yet look up at Rajeev. It processed the voice it had just heard as if it was a remnant from a long-forgotten dream.

"Rajeev?" Natalie's voice, soft and mellifluous, flowed out of the android's mouth.

"Yeah, it's me," he said. "Hi Natalie."

She leapt off the couch; the book fell to the floor. "What are you doing here? What happened? Did they catch you? What the hell!"

He refused to say anything until she sat back down. Once she was settled, he took a seat beside her. His first inclination was to lie; to claim that he had, indeed, been caught by his son's operatives. If it had been any of the other androids seated next to him, he may have said exactly that. But for some reason, Natalie was able to draw the truth out of him.

"I escaped," he said. "It was all going fine. They took me to some grad student's place, a programming whiz, and he was able to disable the failsafe so I could move again. Then they took me to my daughter's . . . wife's . . . house. But they found me there."

"Who found you? NLT?"

"No. Fresh Meat."

"Fresh Meat? But how would they—*why* would they—"

"They knew I was Dev's son. I don't know *how* they knew, but they did. And they wanted to use me to get information on NLT. They asked me to crawl back here and gather any information I could find—any information they could use to rid themselves of their strongest competition."

Natalie nodded her head encouragingly.

"It makes sense for them to come to you. 'The enemy of my enemy is my friend.'"

Rajeev shook his head. "Fresh Meat is arguably even more repugnant than NLT."

"So you refused to spy for them?"

Rajeev hesitated. "They threatened my family. I had no choice."

Natalie reached out and placed her arm on his knee. "Oh, Rajeev. I'm sorry. That's terrible."

"I didn't know what else to do. If I want to keep my family safe I have to at least look like I'm making an effort to spy on my son." Talking about it now exposed emotions Rajeev hadn't even realized were bubbling beneath the surface. If he'd had eyes, they would have teared up. "I didn't want to tell this to any of you, but . . . I don't know. It feels good to tell someone."

"I'm sure it does." She stood. "I don't know what to tell you, though. It looks like you're screwed."

"Tell me about it."

"It's okay, though. We'll all do what we can to help."

"What do you mean?"

"We'll help you gather any intel we can find."

"I can't ask you guys to do that."

"You didn't have to ask. Besides—any scrutiny we can put on NLT increases our chances of getting out of here. In my opinion, we should focus on taking down NLT and then worry about Fresh Meat. I know you may not ascribe to the notion, but I do, so I'll say it again: 'The enemy of my enemy is my friend.'"

* * *

Natalie promised Rajeev she'd spread the word to the other androids about the need for a secret espionage campaign. In the meantime, they returned to their respective dormitories.

As he lay down on his bed, Rajeev found himself questioning whether any of them would find any useful dirt on the company. Next Level Technologies was a state-of-the-art tech company, likely outfitted with the most advanced security technology known to humankind. The likelihood of a bunch of nobodies in robot bodies discovering anything of significance seemed slim.

Still, he had to try. He couldn't let anything happen to Sarah or Mira. If something *did* happen, he'd never forgive himself. He tried to think of what he could do on his own to gain any useful intel, but nothing came to mind. He hoped the other androids were having better luck.

He came to a conclusion: He wasn't going to get anywhere sitting in his bed staring up at the ceiling. He needed to wander around, even if he didn't have a plan. Maybe he could discover something just by stumbling upon it. He got up, walked to the door and emerged from his dorm hesitantly. He meandered down the building's industrial gray halls, unsure of where to go. He was more familiar with this floor than any of the others, and he hadn't noticed any opportunities for espionage, so he thought he'd be more productive on a different level. Once on the elevator, he studied the floor number buttons, then selected one at random to press: Thirty-five.

The elevator beeped and a robotic voice came over hidden speakers built into its ceiling: "Invalid operation."

"What the hell?" Rajeev pressed the button once more, but again, the same monotone voice came over the speakers: "Invalid operation."

"Daniel?" The virtual assistant appeared in the corner of the elevator.

"Hi Rajeev," he said cheerily. "How can I be of assistance?"

"What's wrong with this elevator?"

Daniel furrowed his brow, suddenly looking concerned. "What seems to be the trouble with it?"

"When I press the floor button," he said, pressing the button for a different floor this time, "I get this message." They listened together as the elevator again announced that Rajeev was attempting an "invalid operation."

"It appears your elevator permissions have been disabled," Daniel said.

"My 'elevator permissions?' What the hell does that mean?"

"Everyone on the Next Level Technologies campus has a radio-frequency identification, or RFID, chip to grant them access to different areas of the campus. It also grants access to the elevators. You and the other androids have the chip built into your bodies. It appears the privileges on your particular RFID chip have been altered, granting you permission to only two floors: the sixth and the twelfth."

"So I have access to my dorm and the entertainment lounge, and that's it."

"And any other amenities found on those two floors. Yes."

"How do I change it back?"

"You can't. Only a system administrator can change these permissions."

A system administrator. Like Dev, probably. His son's words suddenly echoed in his head: *Don't expect to have all the same freedoms you did before.*

So that's what he'd meant. Rajeev wasn't allowed to move about the building as he'd been able to before. That made any kind of substantive corporate espionage impossible.

He had to figure *something* out, though, because failure wasn't an option if he wanted to keep his family safe.

Twenty-One

D id you already eat?"

He'd slid into bed as quietly as possible, but Sarah had woken up anyway.

"Yeah, I just got some fast food."

She swats him on the arm playfully. Her voice sounds like a faraway whisper as she says, "You need to stop eating that crap. It's going to kill you someday."

He smiles, amused by the childlike demeanor she's taken on in her half-asleep state. "Anything could kill anyone at any time," he says. "Best not to worry about it."

She sits up and rubs some of the sleep out of her eye. She's waking up now and regaining her full faculties. Rajeev knows that can mean only one thing: A serious talk is coming.

"I want you to quit driving," she says.

He lets out an exasperated sigh. "Sarah, we've been over this—"

"I know, but it's taking a toll on this family. You hardly ever see Dev and Mira, and with Mira's grades slipping . . ."

"I told you why her grades were slipping."

"I know. And she suffered in silence for a long time, Rajeev. She didn't come to either of us. And why would she have? You're never here and I'm always busy holding everything else together. She has no one to turn to."

"We have a mortgage. We have two kids—kids that need food and *clothes and, before too long, are going to need college tuition. How do you think we're going to pay for all that if I quit?"*

"We'll make do. I'm not proposing you do nothing, just that you find a job with a better work-life balance, even if it pays less. The kids are getting older. I can get a part-time job; hell, so can Mira! The kids are smart—they'll get scholarships to help pay for school. We can always find ways to make more money. But we can never buy back time with the kids."

He shakes his head. She has a point, he knows that, but he doesn't feel like he can stop the momentum he's built up.

"I'll think about it," he says.

She nods. "That's all I'm asking from you, for now," she says. "But think it over soon. I need you. The kids need you."

He kisses her cheek. "I know," he says. "I need you, too. I love you."

Rajeev kept coming to the same conclusion. He'd never be able to find a solution on his own; that much was certain. He'd barely been able to set up his own phone in the time before his crash, so he'd certainly never be able to navigate any of the newfangled tech that powered the NLT campus now.

But Gregory Maltek probably could—or had someone on staff who could.

Rajeev tasked Daniel with drafting a message to Maltek summarizing the situation and explaining that if he didn't get his permissions restored somehow, his mission was doomed to fail.

The response took longer than Rajeev would have expected, but then, Maltek *was* the CEO of one of the world's fastest-growing corporations; it was a safe assumption he had other things on his plate. Finally, after nearly thirty minutes, Daniel read Maltek's reply.

"Figures they'd tighten security after you escaped," he said. "I have a man on the inside. Give him a couple hours. I'm sure he can help you out."

Rajeev wondered exactly how many men and women Maltek had "on the inside." There was an entire world of corporate espionage out there he'd barely even known existed. He wondered, was this the way companies like Coke and Pepsi, or Microsoft and Apple, operated? It seemed insane that companies would go to such immoral lengths just to line the pockets of their executives and shareholders, yet it happened all the time. It had always been an abstraction to Rajeev, but now it was affecting the fate of not just himself, but everyone he loved.

He returned to his dorm and waited for Maltek's mole to do his thing. He tried not to think about what would happen if the mole failed. Living the rest of his possibly eternal life shuffling back and forth between his dorm and the entertainment lounge was close to what Rajeev imagined hell might be like. How had he wound up in this ridiculous situation? It all came down to the car accident.

Dev had said it wasn't Rajeev's fault, and that might mostly be true. But how could he be sure he wasn't at least partly responsible? He'd been working a lot leading up to the accident. That in and of itself was a regret. It had cut into time he could have spent with his family. He'd missed out on much of Dev and Mira's childhoods. He'd convinced himself he'd work fewer hours in a couple years so he could spend more time with the kids, but of course, he'd never had a chance to; instead of watching his kids grow up, he'd spent fifteen years in a coma.

All he'd cared about back then was money. It wasn't purely out of greed; as an independent contractor for a ridesharing company, he'd needed to maximize his earnings to pay for all the benefits the job lacked, health and dental insurance chief among them.

That was on top of the mortgage, utilities and socking away some money each month for the kids' college fund. There was no doubt he'd been overworked. He'd had close calls before, toward the ends of his shifts, when he was tired and irritable. He'd taken corners a bit too quickly, drifted into an oncoming lane before noticing and darting back into his own. A couple times, he'd found himself drifting off and had had to pull over after dropping off his passenger to get a good ten minutes or more of sleep before venturing home.

No, maybe the accident hadn't been his fault directly. The drunken driver had swerved into his lane, Dev had said. But maybe if he hadn't been so tired and overworked his reflexes would have been sharper. Maybe he could have swerved into a ditch and avoided a head-on collision. Maybe the accident wouldn't have been so bad. Maybe he wouldn't have spent more than a decade in a coma. Maybe his passenger wouldn't have died.

Maybe.

Daniel appeared suddenly, breaking Rajeev's reverie.

"You have a new message from Gregory Maltek," he said. "Would you like to hear it?"

"Yes."

"'Try the elevator now.'"

"That's all it said?"

Daniel nodded.

Well, Rajeev thought, there was no point in delaying the inevitable. He stood, walked out of his dorm and made his way for the elevator. When it opened, he stepped inside. He wished he could have taken a deep breath; the situation seemed to warrant it.

The doors closed and he faced the rows of buttons before him. He reached out and pressed the button for the thirty-fifth floor.

The button lit up and the elevator lurched slightly as it began its descent.

"Looks like it worked," he said. "Here we go."

Twenty-Two

The elevator doors opened onto the thirty-fifth floor. Rajeev peeked his head out the elevator doors to confirm the hallway was empty. When he saw that it was, he stepped out and made his way down the deserted hall, his footsteps gently echoing off the bare walls.

He had no idea what took place in any part of the building save for the entertainment lounge, Dev's office, and his own dorm. He was aware that he was taking a significant risk by wandering around aimlessly. Someone could find him, notify Dev, and that would be the end of his extracurricular activities.

As he rounded the corner, a meeting room came into view. Through the windows, he took in a group of five people seated at a table. Unlike the entertainment lounge, the conference room's windows were not floor-to-ceiling. Rajeev bent down to the floor, got on his synthetic belly, and crawled beneath the windows. It was a difficult motion, one he wasn't used to making in his new body, but he managed to make his way to the far end of the room. When he was clear of the windows, he stood and continued down the hall.

He came to a plain steel-gray door with a dull metal doorknob. There was no indication what might be on the other side. He reached out, grasped the doorknob, and turned it.

It didn't budge.

Rajeev was discouraged, but not deterred. In his youth, he'd picked a fair share of locks. As a fifty-something-year-old man—or at least, as an android with the mind of one—he took no pride in the skills he'd acquired in his wild youth. But he was now grateful for them nonetheless.

There was no deadbolt on the door, just a keyhole on the knob. He didn't have any lockpicking tools with him, but he didn't think this lock required such drastic measures. He'd opened dozens of locked doors in his youth with nothing more than a stiff credit card, and he suspected that was all this particular door required.

There was one major problem, of course: He didn't have a credit card. He didn't have anything. He could head back to the conference room, perhaps—wait for the meeting to let out, sneak in and look around for anything that could work. But that would be risky.

It occurred to him that he did have *one* thing: His body. He identified the stiff plate making up his thigh. He gripped the material firmly and pulled up sharply; it broke off in his hand. He half expected pain to follow, but of course, there wasn't any—one of the perks of being an android.

The edge where he'd broken the material off was jagged, but the other side was flat, perfect for the task at hand. He slid it down the crack between the door and its frame with practiced expertise, then tried turning the knob again. It turned, and the door swung open.

His photosensors instantly adjusted to the low light. As he took in the contents of the small room, disappointment washed over him. A mop bucket sat in the corner. Shelves lined the walls, filled with rubber gloves, rags, sponges.

He had just broken into a janitor's closet. He stood there a moment, shocked and disappointed. But he couldn't let one misstep deter him. He had to keep moving.

Just as he was about to close the door, the sound of approaching footsteps and the murmuring of people talking floated down the hall. He darted into the closet, closing the door part way but leaving it slightly ajar so he could peek out at the passersby.

The voices belonged to a man and a woman. Rajeev thought he recognized them from the conference room. The meeting must have let out.

"Meet me on the sixtieth floor in a half-hour," the woman said.

The man stopped in his tracks and groaned. "I'm supposed to meet with Stacey in an hour. That doesn't give me much time to—"

"Then cancel it, Ian," the woman cut in indignantly. "This is my top priority right now and it should be yours, too."

Ian sighed. "Fine. I'll see you in a half hour."

"Thank you," she said. They continued walking and made their way around the corner, out of sight. "And be discreet, Ian."

Rajeev waited in the closet several moments after they'd left, giving them and the other meeting attendees plenty of time to get as far away as possible. When he was confident the coast was clear, he crept out from behind the door and closed it gently behind him.

He hurried as quietly as possible back to the elevator. He didn't have much time to make it to the sixtieth floor.

Twenty-Three

When he stepped off the elevator, Rajeev heard voices chattering to his right. He made out a trio of people chatting in the hallway. The man and woman he'd overheard from the janitor's closet were not among them, and luckily no one in the group had noticed him step off the elevator. He hurried to the other side of the hallway until he was safely around the corner.

Now what? He had made it to the sixtieth floor undetected, but he had no idea where to go from here. All he knew was that there was something important here—something that apparently necessitated Ian's discretion. Speaking of Ian, he and his female companion should be arriving any moment. It was possible they'd both arrived early and already left for their destination, but if that was the case, he'd just have to wander around hoping to find them.

He peeked around the corner and watched the elevator. If Ian and the woman emerged and walked away from him, he'd follow after them to see where they went. If, on the other hand, they began walking toward him, he'd scurry off in the opposite direction and pray he didn't stumble into anyone.

A couple minutes went by, and the elevator doors opened. Ian stepped out into the hallway alone. He didn't walk away; he just stood there, presumably waiting for the woman. He seemed miffed that she wasn't already there waiting for him. He tapped his foot impatiently and crossed his arms.

He didn't have long to wait, however; a moment later the elevator doors once again opened and the woman emerged. Rajeev braced himself, ready to turn and run in the opposite direction if they began moving toward him. Thankfully, they turned and walked the other way, disappearing around the corner.

He followed after them, scurrying down the hallway but doing his best to minimize the sound of his silicone-covered feet clicking against the concrete floor. The trio that had been chit-chatting was gone, but Rajeev peeked his head around the corner to make sure there weren't any other interlopers. The hallway was empty, save for Ian and the woman walking slowly but steadily away.

Just as they were about to round another corner, Rajeev took chase again. When he came to the corner, he took another peek and saw that they had stopped in front of a door. The woman flashed a keycard against a sensor. A clicking sound reverberated throughout the hall as the door unlocked. She opened it and let Ian pass through first. Then she followed him in and shut the door behind him.

Rajeev ran to the door and tried the handle but, of course, it was locked again. He cursed. The door was thick and appeared to be made of steel. Even so, Rajeev strained his artificial ears, hoping he'd be able to hear something, anything. But there was no sound.

He'd come so far, but it appeared he was now stuck. As good as he was at picking locks, he didn't know a thing about how to disable a lock with an electronic keycard. He knew there was something important behind that door—something that might satisfy Gregory Maltek's thirst for dirt he could use against the company—but there was no way to get to the other side of it.

Maybe this would be enough to satisfy Maltek. Maybe he had other people "on the inside," as he'd put it, who could break into the room and find out what was behind it.

He turned around to head back, and just as he was rounding the corner he bumped into a security guard.

"Pardon me," the guard started, but then he looked up and saw Rajeev's unnatural face staring back at him. There was a moment of stunned silence from both of them; neither one moved a muscle. Then the guard cried out, "What the hell?" Rajeev sprinted past him, running down the empty hallway as fast as his legs could carry him.

The security guard immediately gave chase, but to Rajeev's surprise, his artificial limbs allowed him to run far faster than he'd been able to as a human being. By the time he made it to the elevator and pressed the button to go down, the guard was just rounding the corner. The elevator doors opened; Rajeev stepped through, pressed the button for the twelfth floor, and watched as the doors closed just before the guard could reach them.

It was a surreal sensation, descending in the elevator, completely calm. He'd just run the fastest he'd ever run in his life. In his old body, he would have been completely out of breath—if not dead—but now he didn't even breathe. He was constantly "out of breath," and it had no effect on him. It was the first time he'd been fully aware of the utility of his new body. He'd always considered it lesser than his old one. Less functional. Less desirable. Less aesthetically pleasing. But he was beginning to realize that a nonhuman body could be greater-than. Running quickly was just the tip of the iceberg.

The elevator dinged and the doors opened onto the twelfth floor. He ran to the entertainment lounge, hoping to find someone inside. He wasn't disappointed: A lone android stood inside, looking straight ahead at the television.

Rajeev rushed inside. "Who are you?" he asked.

The android turned and looked at him. When it spoke, it sounded taken aback by the abruptness of Rajeev's query.

"It's me," he said. "Ted."

"I don't have a lot of time," Rajeev said, speaking quickly. "I found something on the sixtieth floor. I don't know what, exactly, but it's gotta be something big. When you get off the elevators, take a right, then another right. The first door on your left—whatever it is, it's behind that door. I couldn't get inside." Ted was looking over his shoulder; Rajeev turned around and, through the window, saw the guard approaching the lounge. "You need a keycode or something to get in. You guys need to find out what's on the other side of that door, Ted."

The door to the lounge creaked open and the guard barged in.

"Which one of you did I catch sneaking around?" he barked.

Rajeev raised his arms as if a gun was being pointed at him. "It was me," he said. "I'll come quietly."

The guard grabbed him by the arm and dragged him out of the room. Rajeev turned to Ted and gave him one last look. He hoped that despite possessing two dead photoelectric eyes, Ted would be able to see the desperation he meant to convey.

Twenty-Four

Rajeev had known that if he wandered around long enough he was bound to get caught eventually. The humiliation stung all the more, however, because he'd been so close to getting away with it.

He was screwed now. He was sure of it. Ted and the others were his only hope now. If they could somehow get into the room on the sixtieth floor, he was confident whatever was inside would be more than enough to make Greg Maltek happy. Hopefully he'd honor the agreement they'd made and refrain from harming Sarah or Mira. Or Dev, for that matter, although Rajeev was pretty sure his son would consider the resulting damage to his company "harm." He wondered if Dev would ever forgive him once he inevitably found out his own father had betrayed him.

The guard had dragged him into what looked like an interrogation room. A large table took up most of it; a chair sat on either side, and a large mirror made up most of the back wall.

"Wait here," the guard snapped, not even giving Rajeev a chance to sit down before he'd gone and closed the door behind him. Rajeev walked around to the far side of the table and sat.

A few minutes later the door opened again and the guard walked in, followed by Dev. His face was stern, though not angry, which Rajeev counted as a win.

"Leave us, please," Dev told the guard. He did as his boss commanded, glaring at Rajeev the entire time until he disappeared out the door.

Dev took the seat across from his father. He looked him up and down appraisingly.

"You really do have a big pair of balls on you, don't you?"

"Dev . . . let me explain."

"No, let me explain something to *you*, dad. Do you think I'm an idiot? Do you think I'm stupid enough to think it's perfectly innocent that you were somehow able to travel onto unauthorized floors, snooping around in areas that are none of your business?"

"I'm sorry if you feel disrespected, Dev. But I only did it to protect you, your mother and Mira."

"Don't drag them into this. This is about me and you."

"No, Dev, you don't understand. I had to protect you all from—"

"You had to test me," he snapped. "That's what this was all about from the beginning for you. You're used to being the parent, the one in charge, and when you woke up from your coma and found your son in charge of you, you couldn't accept it with humility and grace like a normal person—you had to rebel like a snot-nosed teenager."

"Dev!" He'd raised his voice more than he'd meant to. He sounded, indeed, like a frustrated parent trying to talk over a child in the midst of a meltdown. But he had to get through to his son. He realized that what he was about to tell him could jeopardize everything, but it seemed time to bring his son in on all that had transpired with Gregory Maltek. "Listen to me, Dev. All that I've done, I've done to protect you, okay? Listen to me. Your life, and the life of your mother and sister, were threatened by Fresh Meat."

Dev stopped. He tilted his head. "Fresh Meat?"

"Yes. When I escaped, Gregory Maltek contacted me and made

it clear that unless I came back and spied for him, he would harm you, or Mira, or your mother—anyone I cared about. He wanted dirt on your company, at any cost."

"So not *everything* you've done was to protect me," Dev said, an air of suspicion to his voice. "You left the first time on your own, without any coercion from Gregory Maltek."

"Yes, okay, Dev—I had a moral disagreement about the way you've chosen to run your business. I escaped with the intention of bringing awareness to your company's failings. It was never to hurt you, Dev. I hoped you'd see the error of your ways and change. But that's all irrelevant now, because all that matters right here, right now, is that unless I give Gregory Maltek some juicy piece of intel in the next couple of days, he's going to hurt your mom, or your sister, or both."

Dev grew somber. He looked down at his feet. "I wasn't aware of that," he said.

"I know. But you know now and we need to do something to protect them. Surely you of all people have the resources to keep them safe."

"I do, but I'm not sure they'd accept my help. I'm not exactly on speaking terms with either of them these days."

"Family forgives. Reach out to them. This can be the start of making amends."

He nodded. "Okay. I'll talk to them. But right now, I need you to tell me everything that happened between you and Maltek. Don't leave out a single detail."

Rajeev told the story, explaining how Maltek had sent a representative to Rosa's house. How he'd flown him out to Fresh Meat's headquarters and made him an offer—dirt on NLT in exchange for a boatload of cash and a flesh-and-blood body. How he'd refused, then been given a new offer he couldn't refuse: Dirt on

NLT in exchange for his family's safety.

He went further, explaining how Maltek claimed he had a mole in NLT, and how that mole had been the one to disable his access permissions.

"Wait," Dev interrupted. "If Maltek already has a mole in the company, why did he need you to spy for him?"

"I hadn't thought much about it. My best guess is that his existing mole wasn't entirely effective. I think Maltek thought that because I'm your father, I'd be able to get closer to you and dig up deeper dirt."

"He probably wasn't wrong." He stood and gave his father a grave look. "I want to show you something, dad. I've known for awhile now that Maltek had a mole in the company. Unfortunately, they didn't stop at spying . . . they also engaged in sabotage. I didn't want to involve any more people in this than necessary, but you're in it pretty deeply now and you just may be able to help."

Twenty-Five

D ev led him to the elevator and down to the fifty-second floor. They walked to the end of the hall and came to a heavy steel door. Dev flashed a keycard against a pad attached to the wall and the door opened.

They walked through and Rajeev found himself surrounded by large flat-screen monitors mounted to the walls. Dev closed the door behind him and pointed to a rolling office chair, gesturing for his father to take a seat. Dev turned to the array of electronics surrounding them and raised his hands.

"This," he said with a circus ringmaster's flair, "is what I like to call The Hub."

"It looks impressive . . . but what is it?"

"The Hub is the storage center for all Next Level Technologies' trade secrets," he said. "All the company's vital information is stored here. Our processes for duplicating minds, our robotics technologies, plans for future tech . . . it's all right here. But I can't access any of it."

"Why not?"

"Maltek's mole." He let out a deep sigh and shook his head slowly, as if he had become completely devoid of all hope. "I don't really trust anyone but myself. I placed safeguards on all this information so it could only be accessed by me or with my permission. There are a variety of different kinds of safeguards built in . . . biometric markers—fingerprints, retina scans—as well as passwords, two-factor authentication and security questions. The mole knew they'd never be able to break through all these safeguards, so they stooped to sabotage instead."

"But it all looks operational to me."

Dev shook his head. "It's not The Hub that the mole sabotaged. It's me."

"What do you mean?"

"I've been having memory problems. It started small at first . . . forgetting where I placed my keys, forgetting people's names, that kind of thing. But it got more severe. I couldn't remember discussions I'd had with people just a week prior. I spoke with Mira on the phone once and could only remember her name with significant effort. One day, about two years ago, I needed to access The Hub and couldn't remember the answers to the security questions. I was completely locked out."

"There isn't a way to bypass the questions?"

"No. Every requirement must be met to access The Hub."

"But what if you were to die? Anyone other than you would be locked out of the system."

Dev nodded. "There are definite downsides to my paranoia. I didn't think everything through."

"What do your memory problems have to do with the mole in your company?"

"I have reason to believe the mole has been poisoning me with the express purpose of impairing my memory and preventing me from accessing The Hub."

"Now you *really* sound paranoid."

Dev grinned. "A wise man once said, 'It's not paranoia if they're really out to get you.'"

"But what evidence do you have?"

"Medical evidence. When I began suspecting something was wrong, I saw a doctor. He did some tests and discovered trace amounts of a unique, patented compound in my blood—a compound known to cause memory recall issues. And the patent-holder for that compound happens to be Cyrus Pharmaceuticals . . . a subsidiary of Fresh Meat. Perhaps you think it's a coincidence, but I say it's evidence. There's no doubt in my mind that the mole poisoned me."

"You said you could use my help. What do you expect me to do?"

"Like I said, the only safeguards I'm having difficulty with are the security questions and the passwords. I'm not having any trouble with the biometrics or the two-factor authentication, obviously. But for the life of me I can't remember everything else. I didn't want to bring anyone else into this mess, but now that you're in, you can serve as the memory I've lost."

"You want me to figure out the answers to your secret questions."

He nodded. "And the passwords. There are hints that should be enough to get us in."

"Okay. Let's hear one and I'll see what I can do."

Dev grinned. "Let me see here . . ." He found a keyboard and began typing, bringing up a question on the screen directly in front of them.

"Here's one," he said, pointing at the screen. The security question read, "What is the name of your favorite book?"

"Your grandfather would have hoped the answer would be the *Baghavad Gita*," Rajeev said. "But I don't know the answer to that one, Dev."

"It won't hurt to try . . ." He typed in "Baghavad Gita," but when he hit enter, he was informed that the response was incorrect.

"Throw out some other ideas."

"You should at least have an idea, shouldn't you?"

"I've tried everything I could think of, but nothing worked."

Rajeev fell silent as he racked his brain for the titles of any books that might have had significance in Dev's life. Only one title came to mind, but it couldn't possibly be correct. Still, in Dev's words, it wouldn't hurt to try.

"When you were a child," Rajeev said, "you always wanted me to read you 'Goodnight Moon' at bedtime. I think I must have read you that book for a year straight."

Dev nodded and smiled. "Of course," he said. He typed in "Goodnight Moon," and the screen moved on to another question. "Amazing, dad. Thank you."

"What's the next question?"

"This one doesn't make much sense to me," Dev said. "I'm not married."

The question read, "Where did you meet your spouse?"

Rajeev placed a hand on his chin. "No, you're not. But I don't think that's the point of the question."

"Then what is?"

"Arranged marriage. When you were young, your grandparents held out hope that Sarah and I would arrange a marriage for you kids, even though she and I hadn't even taken that path to our own relationship. Your grandfather always joked that you should marry a little Indian girl, the granddaughter of one of the residents in their housing community. Her name was Amara, I believe."

"That's good, dad! But the answer can't be Chicago—I've already tried it." He put his hand on his chin, contemplating. "Do you remember the name of the housing community?"

"Can't you remember it? You used to visit often enough."

140

"Everything's foggy. I'm counting on you, dad."

Rajeev racked his brain but no clear answer came to him. "How do you know the memory is even in here?" he asked, pointing to his head. "You said you had to fill in a lot of gaps. Surely some of those gaps went unfilled."

"That's a possibility, but it could just be a matter of digging deeper for the information. Think, dad. You might surprise yourself."

He thought a moment more, then came across a name that, for whatever reason, stuck with him. He couldn't be sure it was correct—but what harm was there in trying it out?

"Clairemont," he said. "Try it."

Dev didn't waste a second typing the name into the computer. He hesitated a brief moment, however, before pressing the enter key. They both gazed up at the screen as a green check mark appeared next to the answer.

Dev pumped his fist. "Yes! You're awesome, dad!" The screen briefly changed to an overview of all the security questions with a check mark next to each one, but Dev quickly navigated away.

"It's all here," he said, his voice giddy. He turned around to face his father. "I have full access! I couldn't have done this without your help. What do you say we head up to my office and celebrate—I have something for you that should approximate champagne."

"I appreciate the offer, but no thanks. I'm glad I could help, but I should go. It looks like you have a lot of catching up to do."

"True. We'll celebrate another time."

Rajeev stood and made to leave. Dev turned his attention back to the computer. As Rajeev walked out the door, he heard Dev utter to himself, "Screw Gregory Maltek."

Twenty-Six

As soon as Rajeev was safely inside the elevator, he summoned Daniel.

"What can I do for—"

"Daniel, is everything I see recorded?"

"I'm not sure I understand your question."

"My eyes are basically video cameras, right? So are the images they pick up stored anywhere? Can they be played back?"

"Ah, I see what you mean. Yes, the images are stored anywhere between eight to seventy-two hours, depending on the user settings."

"That's more than enough. How do I bring up the footage for review?"

"I can do that for you. It appears your settings are configured to record and store up to eight hours of footage."

"I just need footage from the past twenty minutes."

"Very well."

A small rectangle appeared in front of Rajeev, appearing to hover about five feet in front of him at eye level. It began playing footage from Rajeev's perspective, showing him walking down the hall with Dev toward The Hub.

"Is there any way to speed this up?"

"Sure," Daniel replied cheerily. Almost instantly, the footage began playing at double speed. Rajeev was afraid he'd miss the moment he was looking for, but he saw it coming.

"Stop!" He shouted. "Play it at normal speed." The footage returned to normal.

"Clairemont," he said in the recording. "Try it." He watched as Dev entered the name into the computer. When it worked, Dev pumped his fist and told Rajeev he was awesome.

"Freeze the picture," Rajeev said. The recording froze, displaying the computer screen Dev had been working with.

"Can you zoom in on the text displayed on the screen?"

"Sure," Daniel said, and the picture magnified. It was a list of all the security questions Dev had had to answer. At the top of the list were the two questions Dev had successfully answered before calling Rajeev in for help:

WHERE DID YOU HAVE YOUR FIRST KISS?

WHAT WAS YOUR FAVORITE PLACE TO TRAVEL TO AS A CHILD?

Rajeev thought back to his conversation with Dev in his office; the one where he'd given him the experimental orb that was supposed to taste like Scotch. He'd casually brought up his childhood. He'd asked Rajeev if he remembered hearing about Dev's first kiss. He hadn't. But then he'd asked about his favorite place as a child, and Rajeev had handed him the answer on a silver platter.

Alarm bells rang like crazy in Rajeev's head. His mind reeled as he tried to figure out what to do. Because he was fairly certain the man back there claiming to be Dev was not his son. And whoever he was, Rajeev had just helped him unlock the keys to all of Next Level Technologies' most closely guarded secrets.

* * *

Rajeev hurried to the entertainment lounge, eager to speak with one of the other androids to ensure he wasn't as crazy as he seemed even to himself.

Three of the androids were huddled together by the couch, talking among themselves. Rajeev walked through the doors and approached them.

"It's me—Rajeev."

"Hey," one of them said. "Ted."

"Brian."

"Natalie."

Good. His most important allies were here.

"I have some big news," he said.

Natalie glanced at her compatriots and nodded. "So do we."

That surprised him, but he couldn't imagine anything they might say could be more revelatory than what he was about to unload on them.

"Okay," he said. "You go first."

"That room you found on the sixtieth floor—I found it," Ted said.

Rajeev had forgotten all about the room. Now, given what he knew about Dev, or whoever was passing himself off as Dev, it seemed like the least of their concerns. But he encouraged Ted anyway.

"Did you get into it?"

Ted nodded.

"What did you find?"

He hesitated. "I think it would be best if you saw it with your own eyes."

Rajeev shook his head. "We don't have time for that. The man I've been calling my son is an imposter. He isn't Dev."

Ted glanced at Natalie, then turned back to Rajeev. "We know."

"You—you know? How?"

"Like I said," Ted answered, moving toward the door, "you really need to see for yourself."

He walked out the door without another word. Rajeev turned to Natalie as if appealing for help, but she just nodded her head toward the door. "He's right," she said. "Go."

He sped out the door, hurrying to catch up to Ted. When he'd caught up, Ted had just pressed the button for the elevator. It was already on their floor, and the door opened immediately.

"Shouldn't we wait for the others?" Rajeev asked as they stepped inside.

"They're not coming. It'd be too conspicuous to have four of us walking around together."

He pressed the button for the sixtieth floor and they stood in silence as they rose up the building. The elevator dinged, the doors opened, and Ted stepped out, confidently striding away.

"Ted," Rajeev hissed, doing his best to run after him while also moving silently, "be careful—we could get caught."

"I'm over it," Ted said. He continued speeding away, refusing to slow his pace for Rajeev, forcing him to abandon caution if he wanted to keep up.

"What's so important that you don't even care about getting caught?

"You're about to find out."

They rounded the corner and approached the door Rajeev had been unable to penetrate.

"How were you able to disengage the lock?"

"One of the other androids used to be a computer hacker. He came up here and was able to figure out the code. To whit—" He punched a string of six numbers into the keypad and a green light lit up. Ted turned the handle, opened the door and walked inside.

The room was dark and the walls were painted black. It was the antithesis of the all-white room Rajeev had first awoken in. The only light came from a small lamp built into the side of one of the walls.

"What's so important about this place?" Rajeev asked. "It looks like a living space. Like one of our—"

He'd caught sight of the far right corner of the room, where a small bed sat. He'd seen it as soon as he'd walked in, but what he'd missed was the silhouette of a man sitting on the side of it. He was short, with an ample build, and even though his face was obscured by shadows, Rajeev recognized him at once.

"Dev?"

The man stood and took a step forward, letting the low light wash over his face.

"Hi, dad."

"How is this possible?"

He beckoned his father toward the bed. "You'd better have a seat. I'll explain everything."

Twenty-Seven

Although he was sitting on the bed, Rajeev felt like he was floating. Everything about this encounter felt like a dream. After awakening in his new body, seeing his son as a grown man had been a shock. But going through the same sensation all over again was more than a shock. It was unreal.

Ted nodded at Rajeev. "I'm going to give you and your son some privacy," he said. "I'll be right outside the door serving as lookout."

"Thanks, Ted."

Rajeev turned his attention back to Dev, who was apparently finding the situation surreal as well.

"That's really you in there, dad?" He sat on the edge of the bed, his torso turned slightly to face his father, who was sitting beside him. His brow was furrowed in a mix of concern and fascination.

"Kind of. A very close copy."

"Of course. I designed the technology that created the copy."

"I know. But I'm more interested in knowing why there are two of you walking around."

Dev frowned, suddenly angry. "There's only one of me. That other son of a bitch is an imposter."

"But how? He looks *exactly* like you."

"I was naive." He looked away, staring at the wall as if taking in the sight of something in the nonexistent distance. "About two years ago, Greg Maltek called me and demanded a face-to-face meeting. He said he wanted to declare a temporary truce to discuss a possible collaboration. I was skeptical. I had—and still have—grave concerns about the ethics of Maltek's technology. How does he produce the bodies? I don't see how he could do what he does without human cloning, and I don't believe the technology exists to clone a human being without a consciousness—a *soul*. That means he must be erasing a human consciousness to create 'blank' bodies that he can sell. He's a murderer. Or so I suspected."

Rajeev nodded. "I had similar concerns."

"Maltek has always been secretive about his technology, and one of the reasons I agreed to meet with him was because I thought I could persuade him to open up about it. He insisted on meeting at the Fresh Meat headquarters, and I agreed to do so." Dev paused, shaking his head. His posture belied the hopelessness and regret eating him alive from the inside out. "There was no meeting. Not even the pretension of one. I'd brought along security, of course, but as a courtesy to Greg, I asked them to wait outside. I stepped into Maltek's office alone. I was such an idiot. As soon as the door closed, Maltek injected me with something and I was out instantly. When I awoke, I was exactly where we are now—in this room."

"But to what end?"

"I didn't know at first. I thought maybe he'd just kidnapped me in hopes that my absence would cause my company to fall apart without me. But that didn't make sense. There are other people in the company who can run things without me. I wasn't quite sure what Maltek was up to, but I knew it couldn't be good. An orderly visited me three times daily to bring me a hot meal, change the sheets on the bed and make sure I hadn't found a way to kill myself. They'd provided me with a tablet preloaded with movies, music, and books, but no internet access and thus, no ability to contact the outside world. I was a prisoner and I had no idea why.

"Things went on like this for months. I couldn't tell you how many; time had begun to lose all meaning for me. But one day I received a visitor who was not part of the regular rotation of orderlies I'd become accustomed to. The visitor was *me*. At first I thought I must have gone insane from the months of solitary confinement. The man who walked through the door was my exact twin. It was like looking into a mirror. But it soon became apparent that I wasn't crazy. The 'other me' was none other than Gregory Maltek."

Rajeev shook his head. "That's impossible! I met Gregory Maltek at the same time your doppelganger was roaming around here."

"It wasn't the *original* Maltek that confronted me. It was a copy, a duplicate, just like you're a duplicate of my father. But in this case, the original wasn't destroyed. Maltek continued operating his business out of San Francisco even as the copy of his mind was inserted into a brain belonging to a body biologically identical to my own—my clone. I don't know how Maltek got a hold of my DNA, but it wouldn't have been difficult. He could have paid someone to retrieve a coffee cup I'd discarded and collected my saliva off the rim, or paid my hairdresser for a bag of my hair. Regardless of how he obtained it, once he had it, he had everything he needed to create a duplicate body and fill it with his duplicate mind. Once the duplicate arrived here in Chicago, Maltek had the perfect inside man—himself."

Rajeev wished he were capable of throwing up. All the intimate moments he thought he'd had with his son were lies. He'd been communing with one of the vilest, most despicable men he'd ever met—or at least with a copy of that man. All the while, his real son had been locked up here going mad from his imposed solitude.

"Why did Maltek do all this? Why go to such elaborate lengths?"

"He wanted my company. More specifically, he wanted to take out his biggest competitor and keep all the technology I'd developed for himself. That's how it started, anyway. When his duplicate walked in, with *my* face, *my* voice, *my* mannerisms, it was because Maltek had run into roadblocks. I've always been a tad paranoid, but in this instance, my paranoia served me well. I'd hidden all the company's secrets on a secure server. I protected it with several different security measures: biometric scans, passwords, security questions. He'd gotten through the biometric scans with no problem; after all, he's a clone, so his DNA is identical to mine. But, naturally, he couldn't figure out the passwords or the answers to the security questions. He was locked out and needed my help to get in."

Rajeev's stomach sank—or at least, it felt like it had—but he waited for his son to finish the story before telling him about the horrible thing he'd done.

"I refused to help, of course," Dev continued. "He tried to beat it out of me. Getting punched by my doppelganger was undoubtedly the oddest experience of my life . . . and the most painful. I held out for a long time. But a man can only take so much and eventually, I caved. But I only told him the passwords, not the answers to the security questions. He left to see if they worked and vowed to return later for the rest. After he was gone, however, I built up my resolve. When he returned an hour later, I refused to give up any more information and he beat me again. By now he was getting frustrated because he was so close to having everything he needed. But I wouldn't budge and he went too far.

He hit me on the side of the head and knocked me out cold.

"I woke up back in my bed. It must have been hours later. As far as I could tell, I'd received absolutely no medical care. Maltek was gone and my head throbbed like a bitch. It was the perfect excuse. When Maltek returned several hours later, I feigned amnesia. I told him I couldn't even remember who I was, let alone what 'security questions' he was asking about." He chuckled as he said, "I even asked him if he was my evil twin."

Rajeev shook his head. "He couldn't have liked that."

"He didn't. He raged at me. But I think deep down he suspected he really had damaged my memory—he'd hit me extremely hard. When he left, he didn't come back. And I've been here ever since."

Dev paused and Rajeev took the opportunity to confess his sins to his son. "I have something to tell you, Dev. I . . . I've made a terrible mistake."

"It can't be that bad."

"I think I just provided Maltek with all the answers to your security questions."

Dev's face fell. "Okay, maybe it is that bad. What happened?"

Rajeev explained how from the beginning, he'd thought Maltek—the duplicate version—was truly Dev. When he'd returned to Next Level Technologies after escaping, he'd been trying to get back into the good graces of the man he'd thought was his son. And he'd helped him answer the security questions that, up to that point, he'd been unable to answer.

Dev listened to his father's story without interruption, and with no visible reaction. But by the time Rajeev had finished, all color had drained from his face.

"If what you're saying is true, then Maltek has control of The Hub."

"That's what I was afraid of. So how bad is it? What kinds of secrets are stored in The Hub?"

Dev didn't answer at first. He seemed to be gathering his thoughts. When he answered, his voice was low and devoid of emotion, as if he couldn't dare let himself express the despair bubbling beneath the surface.

"It's bad," he said. "Real bad."

Twenty-Eight

Dev led Ted and Rajeev out of the room and down the hall. "I'll tell you more, but first we need to get out of here."

"Yeah, about that," Ted said. "You put GPS trackers on us that make our bodies seize if we try to leave the building." There was more than a hint of resentment in his voice.

Dev shook his head. "That feature was never meant to keep you imprisoned. It was a safety measure meant to protect you. Before we activated the first prototypes, we had no idea how the duplicate minds would react when they awakened in an alien, robotic body. We didn't know if they'd be confused, for example, or if they'd suffer from total or partial amnesia. We thought they might run away in a panic and hurt themselves—run into traffic or worse—so we implemented the failsafe to ensure we could bring them back inside and make sure they were safe until they acclimated to their new bodies. It's no surprise Maltek corrupted its purpose."

"That may be," Rajeev said, "but can you disable it quickly so we can leave?"

"Yeah. I'll find the proper equipment. Follow me."

He led them to the elevator. Thankfully, it was empty. They piled in and journeyed to a lower floor. When the doors opened, he walked down the hall and led them through a door. It appeared to be some kind of laboratory. Electrical equipment, wires and other supplies lined shelves against the wall, but other equipment was strewn about randomly. What concerned Rajeev, however, were three people seated around a table at the right-hand side of the room. They immediately looked up at Dev as he entered, quizzical looks on their faces.

Dev froze, like a deer caught in headlights. But then he straightened his back and pointed at the three employees.

"I need the lab to myself to work on these models," he barked, tilting his head toward Ted and Rajeev. "Give me fifteen minutes."

To Rajeev's astonishment, the three of them stood and walked out of the room. But of course they would. Dev was their boss. They couldn't tell the difference between him and the imposter they'd been working under for so long. When they saw the boss, they did what he said.

"That was weird," Dev said as he closed the door behind him. "I'm not used to bossing people around. I'm out of practice."

"Looked like you did a fine job to me," Ted said. "They didn't even make eye contact with you."

"Which is not a good thing. Who knows how much Maltek has damaged my reputation in my own company." He directed Rajeev and Ted to take a seat, then searched around the room for the items he needed.

"Why is it necessary to leave at all?" Rajeev asked. "You're the founder of the company. Couldn't you just stay here and set things straight—kick out the fake Dev and reclaim your place on the throne, so to speak?"

"It's too much trouble right now," he said as he plucked a laptop off a shelf and walked it to the table. "The company would spiral into all-out chaos. Think about it; no one would really know for sure who was the real me, and while they tried to sort the situation out, it would just distract from the real task at hand: Stopping

Maltek." He walked to another shelf, grabbed a couple cords, and walked them back to the table. He stuck each of the cords in the laptop, then inserted the other ends into the ports at the base of Ted's and Rajeev's necks. "This should just take a minute."

Rajeev was familiar with the procedure, having already gone through it once with Zane. Ted seemed a little nervous; he fidgeted more than usual. But Dev was quick—far quicker than Zane had been, which made sense, considering the bodies were based on his own designs.

"We're good to go," he said, pulling the wires out of their necks.

"Good," Ted said. "I can't wait to get the hell out of here. I'm never coming back."

They left, Rajeev walking on Dev's right side, Ted walking on his left. For once, Rajeev didn't feel the need to sneak around. He was with the company's founder; who would dare question him?

They took the elevator to the ground floor. Rajeev was reminded of his earlier escape as they strolled through the hallway headed for the front entrance. But he had no reason to fear this time. He was with his son, the founder of the company, and he was escaping *with* him rather than *from* him. It would be so much easier to—

His good vibes were cut short as they rounded the corner and Dev came face to face with . . . himself. Or at least, with his doppelganger. They both froze at first, staring at each other in shock. The real Dev was the first to snap out of it, and he shouted to his companions: "Run!"

He darted to the left of his clone and sped down the hallway; Rajeev and Ted took another moment to react, but soon followed suit. Maltek grabbed at Ted's shoulder, but his fingers slid off the smooth silicone skin and he came away empty-handed.

"Stop them!" Maltek cried. He took off after them, but they had gotten a healthy head start; Rajeev and Ted easily caught up to Dev, thanks to the endurance of their artificial bodies, and ran ahead of him. As they rounded the corner, Rajeev was presented with the familiar sight of the security desk overlooking the building's exit.

Two guards stood talking in front of the desk and they looked up in surprise at the commotion of two androids springing down the hallways as if running a marathon, their own CEO in hot pursuit. At the same time, Maltek cried out again, his words echoing into the guards' ears from around the corner: "Stop them!"

One of the guards hesitated; he'd recognized Dev's face rushing toward him, but also recognized his voice coming from around the corner. He didn't know what was going on.

The other guard, however, sprang to action. He lunged toward the trio and, apparently trusting that the failsafe would prevent Rajeev or Dev from leaving the building, focused his attention on Dev. He wrapped his hand around Dev's arm. But before he could do anything else, Dev launched his fist into the guard's chin, causing him to release Dev's arm as he soared backward.

Maltek rounded the corner and made eye contact with the other guard. His eyes blazed with fury as he pointed to the escaping trio and shouted, "Stop them—or you're fired!"

The guard rushed toward them, but Dev and Rajeev had already reached the door. Ted had lagged behind and the guard was just able to catch up to him. He wasn't leaving the fate of his job up to chance; he leapt into the air and tackled Ted, sending them both tumbling to the floor in a heap.

Rajeev, who was now outside, heard the commotion and turned around to see what was going on. When he saw Ted, he made to run back inside.

"No!" Ted shouted. "Go! Leave me!"

Rajeev didn't retreat, but Dev grabbed his arm and pulled him away. "We can't help him, dad. We'll get captured too."

Still, Rajeev hesitated, much to Ted's annoyance: "Get out of here you idiot!"

When their words finally penetrated his frazzled mind, Rajeev turned around. With his son by his side, he flew out into the street, away from Next Level Technologies, a free man once more.

Twenty-Nine

They didn't stop running for fifteen minutes straight. Rajeev could have kept going, but Dev needed to rest before they continued. A wooded area stood off to the side of the road and they took refuge behind a row of trees. Nobody would be able to see them from the road unless they looked carefully.

Dev took a seat on a stump. Rajeev asked him what the plan was.

"There isn't one," he let out between breaths.

"You've been sitting in that room this entire time and you haven't given any thought to what you'd do if you got out?"

"Sure I have. But those thoughts didn't constitute a plan. They were fantasies."

"So what the hell are we supposed to do?"

"First we need to get well away from here. The area's going to be buzzing with NLT personnel on the hunt for us us."

"We're never going to manage that on foot."

"Exactly. We need a ride."

"It's not like we can call a Lyft. Although . . . we could ask Daniel to make a call for us."

Dev wrinkled his brow. "Daniel? You mean the AI assistant?"

"Yeah. He could call Mira for us, tell her to come pick us up. Is there any reason we shouldn't? Would Maltek be able to trace the call?"

"He shouldn't be able to. I severed the company's ties to you when I disabled the failsafe. You're invisible to them."

"Okay. Daniel? We need you."

The assistant appeared in front of them; of course, Dev couldn't see him.

"Daniel, can you call my daughter, Mira?"

"Let me check your contact list . . . Mira Sundaram? Is that who you'd like to call?"

"Yes."

"Okay. One moment."

Daniel went silent for a moment; the line must have been ringing, but suddenly he opened his mouth and Mira's voice came out of it: "Hello?"

It was an odd thing, hearing Mira's soft, feminine voice emanating from the mouth of a masculine representation—but there was no time to dwell on it.

"Hi Mira. It's dad."

"Dad? Where the hell have you been? I've been worried sick about you!"

"It's a long story. Look, I'm with your brother maybe a quarter of a mile outside the NLT campus. We need a ride."

"You're with Dev? Why doesn't he just call one of his limos down there and—"

"Mira, it's complicated. Please, can you come? We're desperate here. We'll explain everything in person."

She sighed. "Fine. You're lucky I love you."

Rajeev gave Mira a more detailed description of their location. Then the call ended, Daniel went away and Rajeev turned to his son.

"She's on her way. She should be here in less than a half hour."

"Hopefully we won't get caught before then."

"Hopefully not." Rajeev hesitated, but then shook his head; now was as good a time as any to have this conversation. "Dev, I owe you an apology."

"For what?"

"For not being there for you. Ever. When you were a kid, I worked all the time. I was trying to support our family, trying to give you kids nice things and good opportunities. I think in the back of my head I always figured I'd have an opportunity to slow down later and then I'd make up for lost time and spend more time with you and your sister. But it didn't work out that way, obviously. I was gone for fifteen years and it was because I overworked myself. If I'd gotten more sleep, been more refreshed, then my reaction time would have been faster and I could have—" He cut himself off, overwhelmed by emotions that couldn't be expressed through tears.

Dev had no such limitation, however, and tears had formed in his eyes. His voice trembled as he spoke. "I'm not going to lie and say it wasn't difficult growing up without you. But even if you didn't spend enough time with us as kids, you were still raising us, shaping us through your example. You demonstrated the value of hard work. And it was never lost on us for a *moment* that it was all for our sake. You may question your devotion to your family, dad, but we never did."

Rajeev wanted to cry. Not being able to outwardly express his inner emotional turmoil somehow made the emotions even stronger.

"So you . . . you forgive me?"

"Of course, dad." Dev stood, walked to his father and wrapped both arms tightly around his thin, synthetic torso. Rajeev did the same, holding his son tightly, though taking care not to hold him *too* tight, since even now he wasn't fully aware of his new body's strength.

"I was afraid when I woke up in this body," he told his son as they ended their embrace. "When I learned I was a duplicate of the original Rajeev, I was angry. It felt like I'd been duped into entering the world."

Dev nodded sympathetically. "It was never my intention to create duplicate consciousnesses without the consent of the original individual. You were an exception. I duplicated your consciousness after you were already gone because you were my dad and I . . . I wanted you back. Obviously. But I couldn't get past the ethical questions. I could never bring myself to use it. Maltek must have seen your consciousness on file and figured he could use you to help answer the security questions he still needed. So he uploaded you into an android body and, well . . . here you are."

"And despite my earlier misgivings, I'm *glad* I'm here, Dev. I may only be a carbon copy of the original, but I'm imbued with the same attributes as the original Rajeev Sundaram and the most overwhelming part of him—and thus, of me—is a sense of unlimited love for you, your sister and your mother. I'm glad I'm here, not for my sake, but for yours. I want you to have a relationship with the father you never really knew. I want us both to have a second chance."

Dev nodded. "I appreciate that. And now that you've been activated, where you go from here is up to you." He paused and his face grew dark. He turned away slightly, seeming to peer past Rajeev deep into the heart of the forest. "That is, if we're able to stop Maltek. If we don't, there may not be a future for either of us."

"At Next Level Technologies, you mean."

Dev shook his head. "No. The fate of the entire world hangs in the balance. I know I sound like a dramatic movie trailer announcer, but it's the truth."

"What do you mean?"

"Maltek told me everything. It was when he was trying to torture me into giving him the answers to the security questions. He was taunting me, but I know what he told me was the truth. See, as far as the public knows, Fresh Meat is designing simple replacement bodies that allow people to live forever. There's nothing special about them; they're simply healthy young bodies that allow their customers to be whoever they want to be. But behind the scenes, Fresh Meat hasn't just been making copies of people. They've been augmenting. Enhancing. They're creating superhumans."

"So they're planning to create a new class of human being. Get people to pay more for the deluxe model."

Dev shook his head. "I wish it were that simple. Maltek doesn't just have market domination in mind. He's after *world* domination."

"So the enhanced clones . . ."

"He's building an army of them. He's creating human beings that are faster, smarter, and stronger than any naturally-born human being. *That's* why he went after Next Level Technologies. Not because he thought we'd beat him in the marketplace, but because he knew we had the capability of building our *own* army—one that would be able to stop his. By making that army his own, he not only neutralized the greatest threat to his success; he also strengthened his own forces substantially."

"But how would NLT be capable of countering Maltek's army? I mean . . . look at these things," he said, gesturing toward his body. "I'll admit I have greater endurance than I ever had in my old body, but other than that, I don't see how I could go toe-to-toe with a superhuman."

"Your body was just our first prototype. It was only ever meant to be a test of the interface between the duplicate minds and our hardware. But we had plans for artificial bodies much more complex than what you occupy now."

"So you had more advanced models in the works—stronger, more powerful models, I'm assuming—that could stop Maltek's superhumans. And I'm assuming the plans for those next-generation models were all stored in The Hub?"

Dev nodded solemnly.

"So he has access to all of it. He has an army of superhumans *and* androids."

"He does. And we have to fight back."

"But how can we?"

"I'll show you."

Thirty

The barista is just handing him his coffee when his phone goes off. He's getting a new pickup request.

He thanks the barista, places the coffee in the cupholder, and pulls out of the drive-thru and into a parking space. He glances at the information on the phone: The customer is five minutes away, her destination is about six miles away, and the estimated driver earnings are ten bucks. He accepts the trip. He sips his coffee as he drives to the customer, debating in his head whether he'll make this the last fare of the night or try for a couple more. He's starting to get tired, but if he pushes himself he can make it a two-hundred dollar day.

The navigation leads him to a dingy dive bar on the outskirts of town. He pulls into the parking lot and idles. No one's outside, but just as he's about to call the customer, the door at the front of the bar opens and a young woman walks out and makes a beeline for his car. She's short, with a cherubic face and long brunette hair. She wears a tight-fitting jean jacket, a bright blue T-shirt and black leggings.

She opens the passenger-side door. "Rajeev?"

"Yes. And you are?"

"Samantha." He checks the name on the app: Samantha.

"How are you tonight?" he asks as he confirms the trip on the app and pulls up the navigation to her destination.

"I'm fine. Just getting off work. How about you? Busy night?"

He shrugs. "No busier than usual, but I haven't had much trouble getting fares." He turns on the radio and lowers the volume to background-music status. He always sets it to a smooth jazz station when he's working. The relaxing music helps keep him from going insane.

The obligatory introductory chit-chat subsides and they drive in silence. It begins raining, just a trickle at first, then steady, then pouring. Rajeev drives onto the freeway, windshield wipers pounding at full speed.

"This is some crazy weather," he says. He has to talk more loudly than normal due to the din of the rain plinking against the roof of the car.

"I know. I thought we were done with rain for the season."

"Me too." He turns the radio off; even on a low volume, he finds it distracting with the road conditions requiring so much extra attention. The roads are slick, the sky is dark, and Rajeev recognizes the combination as a recipe for disaster.

The car hydroplanes for a split second, but he manages to steer out of it. He turns his head slightly and apologizes.

"No, it's not your fault," Samantha says. "This rain is horrible. What do you think, should we take the next exit and wait it out?"

"That's up to you. It's your dime. Part of the fare calculation is based on time."

"I'd rather pay a little more than wind up dead."

Rajeev shrugs. "Suit yourself. I'll—"

It happens faster than he can perceive. A pair of headlights that had been safely in one of the opposite lanes is suddenly blinding him. It overpowers his vision completely. He has just enough time to feel a mix of panic and overwhelming regret, and then everything fades to black.

Mira picked them up a few moments later. Dev insisted he

and Rajeev ride in the trunk until they were well outside NLT's proximity, lest any of Maltek's goons spot them and take chase. After driving for about a half hour, Mira pulled into her driveway and popped open the trunk.

"Hurry up and get out of there," she hissed. "If any of my neighbors see you getting out of my trunk they'll be whispering about me for years."

They climbed out and followed Mira into the house. Dev and Rajeev took a seat on the couch as Mira closed the door behind her and turned to face her brother.

"I hope you've come to apologize. Because if you think I'm just going to forget the way you've treated mom and I, you're wrong. You're a selfish brat."

Dev looked flustered and didn't know how to respond. Rajeev stepped in.

"It wasn't him. Your brother has been in captivity this entire time. The person who's wronged you, and who owes you an apology, is Gregory Maltek."

Mira frowned. "What are you talking about?"

Dev and Rajeev took turns telling her the story. By the time they were done, her face was ashen.

"I guess I'm the one who owes you an apology, Dev. I'm sorry. I never should have doubted you. I should have known it was that piece of—"

"Mira, it's okay. There's no way you could have known."

She shook her head. "I still feel badly." She sighed. "Well, what do we do now?"

Dev stood. "Dad, get some clothes on so you can blend in. Mira, you're going to have to take us on another drive." He smiled. "I still have a few aces up my sleeve. Maltek thinks he's going to start a war without any resistance. He's wrong."

* * *

"You're not taking us out here to kill us, are you?" Mira asked.

Dev had directed her to drive out to the Huron-Manistee National Forests, located more than four hours away in Michigan. It was far longer than she'd anticipated driving and she was growing restless.

"No," Dev answered. "It was the only place within a reasonable range of NLT headquarters where I felt I could adequately conceal something of this scope."

"So tell us what we're driving out to see."

"Trust me, it'll be better if I just show you."

For the past three and a half hours, Mira had begged her younger brother to tell her what was so important that they had to drive four hours to see it, but he was resolute, insisting that whatever it was, they had to see it with their own eyes.

Rajeev, meanwhile, was doing his best to suppress his fatherly instincts. In many ways, it felt like taking a roadtrip with the two of them when they were just kids. He felt a pang of regret. Both Dev and Mira had forgiven him for not being there through much of their childhoods, but he hadn't forgiven himself yet. Those moments were lost to him now and he could never have them back. But he was grateful that Dev's technology had given him the opportunity to reconnect with his children. As the old saying went, "Better late than never." He tried to suppress the melancholy he was feeling and embrace the joy he felt at being afforded the opportunity to hear his children bicker once again.

"I love you," he found himself saying.

Mira laughed. "Dad, what are you talking about?"

"Can't a father tell his children he loves them?"

"Of course, but why blurt it out so randomly?"

"I was just thinking about what you two were like as children, and how lucky I am to see how you've both turned out, even after everything that's happened. I may not be the original Rajeev, but as his successor, I'm glad we've had the chance to reconnect. I love you and I wanted to make sure you knew."

"We've always known, dad," Dev said.

"Then I wanted to make sure it was affirmed."

Dev nodded. "I love you too, dad."

"I love you," Mira said. "*Of course* I love you, you dolt."

Rajeev smiled. "I'm glad we've established that we all love each other. I'll refrain from embarrassing you further for now."

Before long, they arrived at the outskirts of the forest. Dev directed Mira down the rural forest roads; her economy car struggled along and the trio felt every bump along the way. Just when Mira felt her car couldn't take any more of the undeveloped dirt roads, Dev pointed excitedly toward a turnoff a few yards away.

"Pull over. This is it."

She pulled into the turnoff and they exited the car. Dev began walking into the woods; Rajeev and Mira just looked at each other.

Dev turned around and waved his arm. "Come on."

"It's a little strange to be luring us out into the middle of the woods like this, especially when we have no idea why," Rajeev said.

Mira turned to her father and nodded. "I know, right?"

"We're almost there. Don't act like you're content to come all this way for nothing." He turned and continued on his path into the woods. Rajeev looked to Mira. She shrugged and followed after her brother. Rajeev took up the rear.

After walking for a few minutes they came across a concrete structure sticking out of the ground like some dull gray monolith.

Dev walked up to it and inputted a string of characters into a keypad at the side of a small steel door built into the structure. He threw his head over his shoulder toward Mira, whose mouth was agape, and Rajeev, who also would have been slack-jawed if he'd had a mouth. "Follow me," he said, and he walked through the doorway and disappeared from sight.

Mira and Rajeev exchanged a look, then walked up and through the door. They found themselves atop a staircase leading into the ground; Dev was already out of sight. They descended, the temperature dropping as they made their way deeper underground. As they neared the bottom, light streamed through a doorway.

As they stepped out of the stairwell, they found themselves in a vast, brightly-lit warehouse, stretching farther than they could see. The walls were made of concrete and reminded Rajeev of the dreary hallways that made up the NLT building. But the warehouse was far from barren. It was lined with seemingly infinite rows filled with equipment Rajeev couldn't begin to understand the purpose of.

Dev stood in front of the sea of shelving, spreading his arms wide, as if everything behind him was a magnificent work of art he'd created and was delighted to show off.

"Welcome," he said, grinning.

"What is this place?" Mira asked.

"This is a storage facility that only I and a handful of close, highly-trusted associates even know exists. There's no mention of it in The Hub. Maltek obviously doesn't know about it, otherwise I'm sure he would have been down here already to empty it out for his own machinations."

"But what is it *for*?" Rajeev asked. "What is all this stuff?"

"Remember how I told you that once Maltek gained control of The Hub, he had access to all of the plans and designs for the next-level tech we planned to create? Well, there's no mention of it in The Hub, but we'd already begun building that next-level tech and this is where we did it. Follow me."

He turned and made his way down one of the rows; Rajeev and Mira followed behind him, taking in the equipment lining the shelves as they walked.

"How were you able to build this place underneath a national forest without anyone knowing?" Mira asked.

"I didn't. We'd contracted with the military, remember? This was their facility. It was already here; had been for decades."

"Wouldn't the military be able to take Maltek out?" Rajeev asked.

"One would hope. But I'm convinced now that Maltek has infiltrated the military, much in the same way he infiltrated NLT—by placing spies that are indistinguishable from the men they replaced. Who knows how high up he's been able to affirm his grip? We can't count on the military. In fact, to be safe, we should assume that the U.S. military is, indeed, under Maltek's thumb."

As he spoke, the rows ended and they walked into an open space that stretched out for another quarter of a mile or so before giving way to more rows of equipment that continued out of sight. Two large pieces of equipment sat against the right wall. Dev approached one, found a foothold and climbed up it.

"This," he said as he made it to the top and lifted a hatch, "is an exoskeleton that increases the strength of a human being fifty-fold. Stay where you are. I'll demonstrate." He dropped into the opening that had appeared when he'd lifted the hatch; a moment later, his hand peeked out and brought the hatch back down.

The mechanism lit up and suddenly unfolded. What had looked like a large, uneven cube suddenly took on the vague shape of a human being. There were two stubby legs attached to two long, flat platforms that served as feet; a stout, square body that also served as a face; and two oval lights making up a pair of slanted, glowing eyes. Thick, riveted arms stretched out from either side. In the center, a clear window showed Dev situated inside what looked like the machine's cerebral cortex.

It was boxy. It was ugly. But there was no question that it was powerful. If there was any doubt, Dev was about to erase it from both Mira's and Rajeev's minds.

The metal beast lurched forward, then lumbered away from the pair of comparatively tiny figures gawking at it, toward the rows of shelving. When it reached its destination, the mechanism's beefy arms reached out and grabbed either side of one of the shelves. Slowly, Dev raised the shelving over his head. The contents slid off onto the concrete floor, the clanging echoing throughout the cavernous warehouse. Dev lifted the shelving triumphantly over his head, then tossed it back onto the ground.

The exoskeleton hobbled back over to Mira and Rajeev. It folded back up into a cube and powered down. A moment later, Dev emerged, a giddy smile smeared across his face.

"So?" he asked as he jumped back to the ground. "What'd you guys think?"

Rajeev nodded. "It's an impressive machine."

"This thing kicks ass!" Mira walked up and placed a hand against the exoskeleton's smooth exterior.

"That's the idea," Dev said. "It'll be kicking Maltek's ass, hopefully. This is our answer to his superhumans. And this is one of the *early* models. We have others that are lighter, quicker and stronger. Gregory Maltek thinks he's going to stage a coup with minimal resistance. He's mistaken. We'll be there to stop him."

"So you really think he's planning to take over?" Rajeev asked.

It was suddenly settling in for him that things were accelerating, coming to blows.

"There's no doubt," he said. He nodded to his father, then again to his sister. "Get ready. A war is coming whether we like it or not. We're going to be here to win it."

To Be Continued In Book Two - Dangerous Minds, coming soon. Read on for a sneak peak of the first two chapters.

Sign up for updates and get a free book—there's no obligation and you can unsubscribe at any time—at www.stevenwyble.com

Remember to leave a review if you enjoyed the book (or even if you didn't ... that's okay too!)

Bonus: Dangerous Minds, Chapter 1

"Mornin', Larry."

Larry looked up from the news story he was reading on his tablet and looked up at his coworker.

"Good morning, Doug. You're late."

Doug glanced at his watch. "Yeah, by two minutes. Screw you, Larry. You're always such a stickler for the rules." The comment had been made in jest, with a smile, but there was a hint of truth to it. Larry was a decade older than Doug and there was no doubt he was far more experienced in the security game. But in Doug's mind, Larry was too rigid—disciplined to a fault. Did the fate of Next Level Technologies really hinge on his being on time, to the minute? He doubted it.

Larry sighed. "Just try to be on time tomorrow. Things have been crazy around here lately, as you know. We need to stay vigilant." The memory of seeing two versions of the company's CEO, Dev Sundaram, was burned into his memory. Unnatural things went on within these walls; things that frightened him. But it was his duty to protect those things and he took the responsibility seriously.

Doug groaned inwardly. Larry sounded paranoid. But there was no point trying to argue with him.

"Yeah, sure. I'll try to be on time."

"Thank you." Larry turned back to his tablet. Doug walked

around to the back of the security desk to clock in.

"What're you reading?"

"A story in the Washington Post. Looks like they might finally fund that hyperloop tunnel in LA."

"Really. We could really use one of those around here. Rush hour is a—"

An explosion clipped his words short; the entire front wall exploded inward, sending dust and debris flying throughout the building's interior.

"Get down!" Larry shouted. But he didn't even wait for his colleague to react; he leapt on top of him, tackling him to the floor. Larry pulled them under the desk, then pulled his shirt over his face and motioned for Doug to do the same. Their chests heaved as they futilely shielded their eyes from the dust with their hands. They both coughed, but once Larry had composed himself, he rose partway to steal a glance into the lobby, trying to make out what had caused the unexpected explosion. Had they had a gas leak or something?

He didn't see anything at first; the dust was still too thick. But as it began to clear, he made out an impossibly large silhouette. It was boxy, and slow moving, but vaguely shaped like a man. It stood at least ten feet tall and nearly as many wide. And it was heading toward them, approaching with a lumbering but powerful movement.

"Shit . . . Doug! Get up!"

Doug was still cowering on the floor and he made no move to get up despite Larry's order.

"What's happening?"

"I don't know. But something is coming right at us—something big."

This, at last, got Doug's attention. He shot up and followed

Larry's gaze. His eyes widened and his jaw fell.

"What the hell is that thing?"

"I don't know. Run ahead and warn Mr. Sundaram. I'll see if I can stop it."

Doug didn't hesitate, skittering off down the hall and out of sight, like a dog running away with its tail between its legs. Larry stood, took a deep breath, and walked out in front of the . . . *thing*, whatever it was. He tried to steel himself for the possibility that this beast would end up killing him.

"Stop!" he shouted, holding up a hand. To his surprise, the monstrosity halted. He stared at it. Dust still hung in the air, but it was clearing to the point that he could get a better look at the thing. It appeared to be some kind of giant robot, but it was nothing like the ones the company was developing inside the very building he was standing in. It was several times larger than the largest human beings. Its arms and legs were as thick as tree trunks. It didn't have hands as much as claws.

Only a fine haze of dust remained in the air and as Larry gazed at the mechanical titan before him, he noticed for the first time a glass window where he'd imagine the chest would be. On the other side of the glass was the faint silhouette of a human operator.

"You can't come through here!" Larry shouted with a hell of a lot more confidence than he felt. He pointed toward the now-missing wall. "Turn around and go back the way you came."

There was a pause, and then a voice came over speakers built into the machine. The voice was vaguely familiar, but Larry couldn't put his finger on it.

"I don't want to hurt you. Please step aside."

Larry gulped. "I can't do that. Now leave. You're trespassing on private property."

"Your commitment to your job and the commensurate duties is

admirable. But I'm afraid I can't leave without my friends."

Larry raised an eyebrow. "Who are your friends?"

"I don't have time to chit-chat. I'm coming through, whether you like it or not." The machine moved forward again, walking slowly but steadily in Larry's direction.

"Oh no you don't." He reached for his waist and his hands gripped the pistol sticking out of the holster on his hip. He raised it, turned the safety off, and pointed it at his oncoming foe.

"Not another step or I'll shoot!"

The machine continued its approach and Larry, being a man of his word, fired a shot. He'd aimed for the glass window—and thus, for the person at the machine's controls—but it must have been made of bulletproof glass, because the bullet merely ricocheted off and came back at him.

The bullet sank into his leg. He cried out and collapsed to the floor, clutching his leg and looking on in horror as the unstoppable machine trudged past him and down the hallway, into the heart of the building.

Keeping one hand pressed to his wound, he used the other to retrieve the radio transmitter secured to the side of his chest. He brought it to his mouth, pressed the button on its side and spoke. "Doug? Have you found Dev?" He waited a moment before continuing, but there was no response. "Doug, I slowed it down a little but I couldn't stop it. It's headed into the building." He paused again. Nothing. "I've been shot in the leg. I need medical assistance as soon as possible. But our first priority is stopping that thing, whatever it is."

He wondered if Doug had dropped his radio. There was no way of knowing—and no assurances that any kind of medical aid would be arriving anytime soon. He retrieved a pocket knife from his trouser pocket and cut off one of his shirtsleeves. He tied it around his leg as a makeshift tourniquet.

He was in a great deal of pain, but he was sure he'd survive. He couldn't walk, however—he couldn't do anything to stop the threat storming through the corporate campus he was supposed to be protecting. He just hoped Doug would rise to the occasion.

Bonus: Dangerous Minds, Chapter 2

Rajeev Sundaram made his way down the hallway of the Next Level Technologies building unsure of where to go. He could head to the entertainment lounge on the twelfth floor, but he wasn't sure it still existed. Gregory Maltek surely hadn't taken kindly to his escape, especially since he'd taken off with Dev, the true owner of the company. It wouldn't be out of character for him to take out his anger on the androids he still controlled.

He had only ever interacted with the other androids in the lounge, but they probably spent most of their time in their individual dormitories—that is, unless Maltek, as an act of vengeance, had banished them to some kind of dungeon or something.

Rajeev's dorm had been on the sixth floor, and he imagined most of the other androids were situated nearby. There was no way he'd be able to fit into the elevator in this monstrous exoskeleton, however—he barely even fit in the hallway. That left only one option.

He looked up at the ceiling. He couldn't see it with his own eyes; the exoskeleton blocked his view. But he was surrounded by video feeds in all directions, so when he looked up, he saw the ceiling as viewed through the cameras atop the exoskeleton's head.

"Here we go," he muttered to himself.

Twin rockets on the bottom of the exoskeleton's feet roared to life. Immediately, the entire mechanism soared upward into the ceiling and broke through into the next floor, plowing through five more until Rajeev turned the rockets off. He fell through the hole in the floor, but quickly stretched out the mechanical arms to stop the fall and climb back onto steady ground.

He stood and looked around, trying to regain his bearings. He spotted the elevator entrance, which helped orient him, and made for his old dormitory. His footsteps thundered down the hall as he went. When he reached the small room, he made to open the door, but the exoskeleton's fist couldn't handle the fine motor functions necessary to turn the doorknob, and slammed the door off its hinges instead.

The room was empty, except for the small bed he'd slept on—a bed that, strictly speaking, wasn't even necessary except as a comfort from his old way of life. He thought maybe another android had been assigned to his old room, but that apparently was not the case.

He turned his attention to the door across the hall. Two large steps were all it took to place him directly in front of it. He swung his right fist into the door, punching it directly down onto the concrete floor. He stepped through.

The dormitory was identical to his own, except mirrored. Sitting on a small bed in the leftmost corner was an android body identical to his own. It was impossible to distinguish one android from another visually, as they all looked the same. They had to rely on each other's voices instead.

"Who are you?" Rajeev shouted.

The android raised its head quizzically. "Rajeev?"

The voice was eminently feminine and Rajeev knew immediately who he was talking to: Natalie.

"Yes, it's me. I don't have time to explain what this is"—he gestured toward the exoskeleton with one of its large claws—"but I'm busting you out of here. Follow me."

He turned and walked back into the hallway. He was surprised to see three other androids already in the hall, apparently checking to see what all the ruckus was after he'd knocked down Natalie's door.

"It's me, Rajeev!" he shouted. "Gather the other androids—as quickly as you can. I'm getting you all out of here!"

The androids took a moment to react, stunned by the situation before them—a bulging, mechanized mess speaking with the voice of a former compatriot—but as the realization set in that this was perhaps their last, best hope of escaping the building that had become their prison, they sprang into action, darting away to gather the others.

Natalie saddled up beside the exoskeleton and looked up at Rajeev. Her stonelike facial expression was unable to convey the sense of wonder she was feeling, but her voice left no doubt she was impressed by what she saw.

"Some upgrade."

"Tell me about it." His voice expressed the smile his face couldn't.

The sound of approaching footsteps broke them out of their reveries. Rajeev braced himself and watched the corner, waiting for his opponents to round it.

"Get behind me," he ordered Natalie. She didn't seem thrilled at being bossed around, but she recognized the gravity of the situation and did as she was told.

A single entity rounded the corner first. He was dressed in black tactical gear, including a helmet with what Rajeev assumed was a bulletproof faceplate. He couldn't tell through all the protective gear whether it was a woman or a man, but he got his answer soon enough when the person opened their mouth.

"Stop!" It was a man's voice, and as he spoke, he raised a gun in his right hand and pointed it squarely at Rajeev. Meanwhile, four other people dressed in the same tactical gear rounded the corner and took up position behind the first man.

"I don't want to hurt you," Rajeev said. "Put down your guns and leave."

"Disengage the machine, and step forward with your hands in the air!" the man called back.

"That's not going to happen. You're going to want to—"

Rajeev's words were cut short by a staccato burst of gunfire. The man had fired four quick, successive shots directly at him. All four bullets found their mark, but the effect was nonexistent. The bullets bounced off the bulletproof glass surrounding Rajeev and fell to the floor with a soft clank. The man looked up at Rajeev with shock and fear on his face, but soon steeled himself and removed any hint of emotion.

"As I was saying," Rajeev continued, "you're going to want to turn around and let me do what I'm gonna do. That is, if you want to live."

The man seemed to waver for a moment. He looked over his shoulder and shared a look with one of the other gunmen, but Rajeev couldn't get a good enough look to tell what he was trying to convey. When he turned back to look in Rajeev's direction, there was an unmistakable resolve in his voice.

"It's my duty to protect this corporation," he said. "You are committing an act of terrorism. I don't know why you're doing it and frankly, I don't care. All I know is that you must be stopped—by any means necessary."

If he'd had lips, Rajeev would have cracked a smile. The man had grit, no doubt. Unfortunately, there was a good chance it was going to get him killed. He'd try to give the man and his team one last opportunity to bow out gracefully—but after that, he couldn't be held responsible for whatever happened.

"This isn't an act of terrorism," he said. "It's a rescue operation."

The man seemed to hesitate, but when he spoke again his voice was steady. "You may think you're doing this for some noble cause, but I assure you, you're nothing but an angel of destruction and we *will* stop you."

"These are human beings," Rajeev said, gesturing with one of his massive arms toward Natalie, who was still behind him, like a small child cowering behind its mother. "They may look like robots, and on the surface, they are. But beneath every one of their metal-and-silicone shells is a human mind, no different from yours. And they are being held here against their will, as slaves. You may consider me a terrorist, but I consider NLT a slaveholding company and I'll do whatever is necessary to free these slaves. If you want to live, I suggest you get out of my way."

The man looked torn. He lowered his weapon and turned around to face the others. For a moment, Rajeev thought he'd successfully deterred the man, but when he turned around again he raised his gun once more and aimed it directly at Rajeev. "Fire on the count of three," he commanded. "Aim for the glass in the center—it can't possibly hold forever. Not with the amount of firepower we're going to throw at it."

Rajeev's heart sank. Despite all his talk, he'd desperately hoped the confrontation wouldn't escalate to this point. He had never taken a human life before and he didn't relish the thought of starting now. But his son, Dev, had insisted a war was coming. There would be deaths soon enough. Lots of them. These were likely to be the first of many; hundreds, if not thousands . . . maybe even millions.

"One!" The man's voice shot through the hallway like a bullet. Rajeev sent the exoskeleton lurching forward as quickly as it could move, which was equivalent to someone walking at a moderate pace. The tactical group remained steady, guns pointed, waiting.

"Two!" Rajeev was getting close; he was near enough now to make out the faces behind the faceplates. He raised one of his massive claws in the air, preparing to bring it down upon the leader's faceplate, smashing out his existence in one fluid motion.

Finally, the leader let out one final cry, one last, desperate command to protect the building he and his men had been charged to serve: "Three!"

About the Author

Steven Wyble is an award-winning journalist, editor and author living in Bremerton, Washington. He is the author of *Metacognition and other stories and poems of science, faith and the supernatural*. *Duplicate Minds* is his first novel—and the first in a planned trilogy.

You can connect with me on:
- http://www.stevenwyble.com
- http://www.twitter.com/asimovman
- http://www.facebook.com/stevenwyble

Subscribe to my newsletter:
- https://tinyurl.com/FreeBookStevenWyble

Also by Steven Wyble

Metacognition

What if time stopped for five billion years? What if we could read each other's thoughts—and what if a select few could also control them? What if you could liquify the air around you and swim through the sky? What if you could change your sexuality? Get in a fight with a glove? Date a raccoon?

The answers to these profound questions—and many more—are nestled within the pages of the book you hold in your hands at this very moment. Gather the courage to explore these pages and discover what it means to be human when science, faith and the supernatural collide.

The Lock

Lena lives an unremarkable life as a barista at an unassuming coffee shop in downtown Seattle. But when she witnesses a man fall to his death outside her shop one night, she's thrust into a world of danger, intrigue and literal monsters.

This is a work in progress. Read it for free on Wattpad at www.tinyurl.com/WattpadTheLock

www.ingramcontent.com/pod-product-compliance
Lightning Source LLC
Chambersburg PA
CBHW050139110726
47898CB00008B/2595